How Can
the Poor
Be Helped?

How Can
the Poor
Be Helped?

Other books in the At Issue series:

At ✳ Issue

How Can the Poor Be Helped?

Geoff Griffin, *Book Editor*

Bruce Glassman, *Vice President*
Bonnie Szumski, *Publisher*
Helen Cothran, *Managing Editor*

GREENHAVEN PRESS
An imprint of Thomson Gale, a part of The Thomson Corporation

THOMSON
™
GALE

Detroit • New York • San Francisco • San Diego • New Haven, Conn.
Waterville, Maine • London • Munich

For more information, contact
Greenhaven Press
27500 Drake Rd.
Farmington Hills, MI 48331-3535
Or you can visit our Internet site at http://www.gale.com

Greenhaven Press anthologies primarily consist of previously published material taken from a variety of sources, including periodicals, books, scholarly journals, newspapers, government documents, and position papers from private and public organizations. These original sources are often edited for length and to ensure their accessibility for a young adult audience. The anthology editors also change the original titles of these works in order to clearly present the main thesis of each viewpoint and to explicitly indicate the opinion presented in the viewpoint. These alterations are made in consideration of both the reading and comprehension levels of a young adult audience. Every effort is made to ensure that Greenhaven Press accurately reflects the original intent of the authors included in this anthology.

Cover credits: © Digital Stock; Photos.com

LIBRARY OF CONGRESS CATALOGING-IN-PUBLICATION DATA

How can the poor be helped? / Geoff Griffin, book editor.
    p. cm. — (At issue)
Includes bibliographical references and index.
    ISBN 0-7377-2717-9 (lib. : alk. paper) — ISBN 0-7377-2718-7 (pbk. : alk. paper)
    1. Poverty. I. Griffin, Geoff. II. At issue (San Diego, Calif.)
HC79.P6H678 2006
362.5—dc22
        2005046234

Printed in the United States of America

Contents

Introduction

According to the most recent data by the U.S. Census Bureau, poverty rates in the United States are rising. In 2003 the official poverty rate was 12.5 percent. This means that 35.9 million people were living below the federal threshold for poverty. Poverty is a serious problem in America, and its society continually straggles with the question of how best to help the poor. Answers to this question, however, depend on how poverty is defined. The government defines poverty as a low level of income and provides assistance to people whose yearly earnings fall below a certain threshold. Many people disagree with this definition, however, arguing that poverty is more than just a lack of money. They maintain that poverty includes being forced to attend substandard schools, the prevalence of families headed by single parents, and an absence of political power. These critics insist that solutions to poverty should thus focus on addressing these factors and others rather than simply on providing financial assistance.

The federal government bases much of its assistance to the poor on its definition of poverty by income levels. This official definition is based on the income of a family in relation to the cost of living. According to the Department of Health and Human Services, in 2005 a family of four was considered to be living in poverty if its yearly combined earnings were $19,350 or less. The poverty line for a family of six was $25,870. This definition is used to determine eligibility for numerous federal assistance programs upon which many poor Americans depend. These programs include Head Start, the Food Stamp Program, the National School Lunch Program, the Low-Income Home Energy Assistance Program, and the Children's Health Insurance Program.

Many people believe, however, that poverty has underlying causes that are more complicated than income levels, and that efforts to reduce poverty must focus on these causes. For example, it is widely believed that a major cause of poverty is poor quality or insufficient education and that efforts to reduce poverty must thus focus on improving education. Statistics show that a low level of education is correlated with a low income. According to the National Center for Children in Poverty, 82 percent of children whose parents do not have a high school diploma live in low-income families, while only 22 percent of children whose parents have at least some college education live in low-income families. Bread for the World Institute, a poverty research organization, argues that improving the U.S. public school system is an effective way to fight poverty. The organization also maintains that having access to higher education helps citizens move up the economic ladder. According to the institute, for every demographic in America—African Americans, whites, Latinos, men and women, and others—incomes rise as education rises. Research by the Cato Institute, a public policy research organization, has shown that for every 1 percent increase in the number of high school graduates in a given population, the poverty rate in that population drops by 1.8 percent.

Others believe poverty is related to single parenthood and a weak family structure. Educator Ruby K. Payne expresses this point of view, noting, "The reality is that financial resources, while extremely important, do not explain the differences in the success with which individuals leave poverty nor the reasons that many stay in poverty." Statistics from the U.S. Census Bureau reveal that families without fathers are also more likely to live in poverty. In 2001 the bureau found that 48.9 percent of children under six years old living in poverty lived with a single mother compared with just 9.2 percent of those who lived with both parents. In light of such statistics, researchers like Robert Rector suggest fighting poverty by providing the poor with parenting classes and marriage counseling that encourage the development of strong, stable families.

Still other people believe that poverty is perpetuated by a lack of political power among the poor. Writer Francisco Unger argues that America's government is dominated by the middle and upper classes who largely ignore the problem of poverty. "We want to believe that our empire is built on foundations of equality and liberty," he says, but the reality is a political system controlled by those with money, who use that power to further their own interests. Journalist James Jennings echoes Unger's conclusion. The real reason for continuing poverty is not that America lacks the resources with which to fight it, he maintains, but the "absence of poor people themselves from the analysis or political resolution of the problem." In *Human Development Re-*

port, a yearly report commissioned by the United Nations to assess and advance human well-being, the authors argue that efforts to reduce poverty must focus on political empowerment of the poor. The report states: "Politics . . . determines what we do—or don't do—to address human poverty. And what is lacking is . . . the political momentum to tackle poverty head on." The authors believe this momentum will be created when those actually in poverty exercise their political power.

As these different theories illustrate, there are many ideas about what causes poverty and how it can best be reduced. One idea that most people do agree on, however, is that poverty is a complex and serious problem that needs to be addressed. The authors in *At Issue: How Can the Poor Be Helped?* offer some suggestions on the most effective ways to approach this continuing problem.

1

Government Programs Will Help America's Poor

Benjamin I. Page and James R. Simmons

Benjamin I. Page is the Gordon Scott Fulcher Professor of Decision Making at Northwestern University and the author or coauthor of several books, including Who Gets What from Government. *James R. Simmons is the chair of the Department of Political Science at the University of Wisconsin in Oshkosh.* Page and Simmons cowrote the book What Government Can Do: Dealing with Poverty and Inequality, *from which the following viewpoint was excerpted.*

The best way to help America's poor is through government programs. There are four ways government can better the lives of the poor. First, the government should assist people in acquiring work skills. Second, the government can try to ensure that well-paying jobs are available. Public service employment, labor unions, and an increase in the minimum wage can assist with this goal. Third, the government should provide health insurance and unemployment insurance for everyone. Finally, the government should guarantee a minimum amount of food, shelter, and medical care to each American.

[W]e ask] what, if anything, government can do about poverty and inequality. Our answer is clear: government can do a great deal. It can do so while preserving other things we value, including liberty, economic efficiency, and general prosperity.

Persistent poverty and a high level of income inequality in the United States cast a dark shadow over our otherwise great achievements. When . . . about one-fifth of American children live in families with incomes below the poverty line, when the top fifth of families receive about half of all the income in the country but the bottom fifth get less than 4 percent of it, something is seriously wrong. No doubt a substantial degree of inequality would be tolerable, so long as the lot of those on the bottom was satisfactory and steadily improving. But that has not been the case. Inequality has increased sharply over the past three decades, with big gains for the wealthy, while most people's incomes stagnated or declined. We are troubled by the extraordinary extent of disparities in income and wealth, by the persistence of absolute poverty, and by the fact that many millions of working people have to struggle desperately in order to make ends meet.

Such extensive poverty and inequality waste lives and cause unnecessary suffering. They limit freedom. They prevent full individual development, impair a sense of community, upset social stability, make a mockery of the idea of equal opportunity, and unnecessarily reduce human happiness.

> *Extensive poverty and inequality waste lives and cause unnecessary suffering.*

Private markets and free-enterprise capitalism, for all their virtues, plainly do not themselves keep the levels of poverty and inequality within acceptable bounds. Even to the extent that markets accurately reward individual skills and efforts—and the most eloquent defenders of markets admit that they do not invariably do so—huge inequalities in "rewards" cannot be considered fair or just. Many factors that lead to high or low incomes are beyond individuals' control. To a great extent, they reflect happy or unhappy chance, the results of nature, nurture, and social arrangements: the fortune or misfortune of genes, upbringing, parents, peers, good breaks, catastrophic accidents, economic fluctuations, global trends.

Nor is poverty or extreme inequality necessary in order to motivate people to learn, to work hard, and to do their best. Duty, pride, love of family, aspirations for achievement, and self-fulfillment are excellent motivators. We do not need to use unlimited greed or fear of starvation. Given encouragement and opportunities—the opportunities are crucial—the vast majority of people will work hard and productively.

> *" Given encouragement and opportunities—the opportunities are crucial—the vast majority of people will work hard and productively. "*

There are many reasons therefore to think that governments *should* act to reduce poverty and inequality, if they can do so in ways that do not entail too many costs: without too much inefficiency, for example, and without seriously infringing on individual liberties. Our review of the evidence indicates that government *can* in fact do so. The old canard that governments cannot do anything right is simply not correct. Nor is the newer claim that globalization renders national governments completely impotent. Yes, globalization does exert pressure against certain types of egalitarian programs, but those pressures are much less overpowering than is often supposed. Some important kinds of egalitarian programs (investment in education, for example; childhood health and nutrition; income supplements for low-wage work) actually can confer global competitive advantages, rather than disadvantages. Yes, it requires creativity and care to design programs to maximize their effectiveness, while minimizing red tape and bureaucratic interference. But such creativity and care are well within the reach of our experts, political leaders, and citizenry.

Right now, in fact, the U.S. federal, state, and local governments *do*, in many efficient and effective ways, contribute to the reduction of poverty and inequality. At the same time, there remains much more that can and should be done. To make further progress requires recognizing and surmounting certain political and economic obstacles. . . .

Preparing People for Work

[There are four ways that government can help the poor.] One fundamental strategy is to *help everyone develop the skills, knowledge, motivation, and physical capability for productive work.* Work should be the cornerstone of efforts to deal with poverty and inequality. Work is central to self-esteem and self-fulfillment. It produces the valuable goods and services that are needed for healthful and satisfying lives. The value of an individual's work will, and should, generally have a substantial relationship to the income received by that individual and her or his family.

A crucial way to reduce poverty and inequality, therefore, is to make sure that very few people are unable to work and that as many people as possible acquire high-level skills and work capacities that are close to those of the most talented and energetic members of society. In a largely market-driven economy, where financial rewards partly reflect the value of what people produce, it would be difficult to proceed very far toward income equality without first working toward more equality of productive capacity.

The strategy of preparing people for work has profound implications for a wide range of government policies, starting at the very origins of people's lives. It suggests, for example, that we need to reduce the chances that children will be born with preventable disabilities or that they will suffer from life-constricting malnutrition, violence, emotional damage, an intellectually deprived home life, or inferior schools. To put it in positive terms, we need to try to ensure that children are born to healthy, loving, and nurturing parents who (along with peers and schools) will provide emotional support, intellectual stimulation, and opportunities for healthy growth and learning.

> *Work should be the cornerstone of efforts to deal with poverty and inequality.*

The excruciating problem is that there are now severe inequalities among the parents, peers, and neighborhood schools that will play critical parts in developing the work capacities— or incapacities—of future citizens. Inequalities among parents, communities, and schools are likely to produce highly unequal work capacities, and highly unequal incomes, in the next generation of children. This means that government policies need not to try to reduce the inequalities among parents and neighborhoods and schools—a formidable and very long-range task—but also to *compensate* for persistent inequalities in children's environments. They need to work from an early age to help provide the nutrition, health care, nurturing, intellectual stimulation, and teaching that children in deprived families and deprived communities may otherwise miss. . . .

Major policy changes are needed before all American children have anything close to equal opportunity to develop high-level work skills and capacities. A really thoroughgoing approach would probably have to include the economic as well as racial desegregation of all U.S. communities and neighborhoods, so that rich and poor people live together and all their children have equal chances to profit from interaction with the most advantaged peers and schoolmates. But such desegregation may not be feasible. It would go directly contrary to the preferences of most high-income people and many in the middle class; it would run up against the sharply income-segregating tendency of private housing markets and the long-term refusal of U.S. public policy to intervene.

> *In both good times and bad, we should encourage, rather than discourage, labor unions and collective bargaining.*

If we continue to refuse to undo the economic apartheid that so strongly tends to perpetuate inequalities, it is important to have open eyes about the consequences. If we want to reduce inequalities without tackling residential segregation by economic class, major compensatory efforts will be needed. For example, to bring schools located in poor neighborhoods (where each student generally needs much more help and attention) up to the quality of schools located in affluent suburbs will require not just equal resources, but *more* resources for each child. Such schools will require not just equal salaries for teachers, for example, but substantially *higher* salaries, in order to encourage the best educators to accept the challenge.

In any case, it is clear that many public policies will have to be changed if we are to move toward the goal of equal preparation for work. The highly successful Head Start program should be further enriched and extended to many more preschoolers, including younger children as well as the many who are now eligible but not funded. Family planning, and health and nutrition programs for children and pregnant women, should be expanded so that children are not born into hopeless situations—and so that the situations that children are born into are not hopeless. The successful vocational education, apprenticeship, job training, and retraining programs need to be expanded. Most important, American public schools—critical foundations for any effort to equalize education and training—should be further strengthened, especially in lower-income communities. They need more resources, better leadership, perhaps carefully designed competition among schools (e.g., charter schools), and special attention to the cognitive skills and information-processing technology that are so highly valued in today's economy.

Ensuring the Availability of Jobs at Good Wages

Even if everyone is willing and able to work, neither poverty nor inequality can be much reduced if people cannot find jobs that pay them enough to live on. The second main strategy for government policy therefore is to try to *ensure that everyone able to work has a job, that the net incomes from all jobs are sufficient for a decent standard of living, and that the net incomes of the highest- and lowest-paid workers are not excessively unequal.* Our focus is on *net* disposable incomes, after all taxes and government transfer payments, because government can use tax and transfer policies to supplement low wages up to an acceptable level and to redistribute part of the highest incomes. Government can also manage the economy so as to raise the level of private wages, and can provide well-paying public service jobs. No one of these approaches is sufficient by itself. All are needed. . . .

Much remains to be done, including making sure that the gains won in good economic times are not squandered in harder times. The benign late-1990s macroeconomic policy of low interest rates, which encouraged substantial economic growth and rising wages, should be continued or restored. Public service employment, usually neglected in boom times, should be in place at all times for those who cannot find private jobs and should be kept available on a standby basis for quick expansion during economic downturns. It would not be difficult to keep an administrative structure in place, along with a prioritized list of public projects to activate in hard times. There are plenty of unmet needs: maintaining and expanding public parks, renovating slum housing, creating works of art, upgrading rapid transit, fixing urban school roofs, blazing forest trails, building and expanding branch libraries. Funding could be automatically triggered by a downturn in economic indicators, and projects could be activated in order of priority.

In both good times and bad, we should encourage, rather than discourage, labor unions and collective bargaining. It is also important to use the twin tools of minimum wage laws and the Earned Income Tax Credit to keep workers' net wages from falling to unacceptably low levels. In order to accomplish this, the minimum wage, which finally began to creep upward in the middle and late 1990s after two decades of decline in value, should be set at a substantial level—perhaps a bit more than one-half of average wages. The minimum wage should automatically rise as workers' productivity increases. The EITC, which is very important for supplementing the incomes of low-wage workers, should be increased so that it, together with the minimum wage, assures that no full-time worker falls below the poverty line. The arbitrary and unconscionable exclusion of childless workers from full EITC benefits should be ended.

> *The present failure of the United States to provide any health insurance at all for some forty-five million of its citizens, a failure that is unique among advanced countries, is scandalous.*

Another important policy change related to net wages would be to make taxes more progressive. In particular, higher amounts of income should be made subject to Social Security payroll taxes (a measure that would greatly enhance the financial health of the Social Security system), and personal income tax rates should be increased on the highest incomes. Since the 1980s, the wealthiest Americans have enjoyed an amazing bonanza of rapidly rising salaries and extraordinary capital gains. Between January 1980 and the end of the 1990s, for example, the average value of blue-chip stocks increased by about *1,200 percent*—that is, stocks became worth about *thirteen times* as much. At the same time that the average worker's wages were stagnating, in other words, a wealthy investor who simply held onto his or her stocks (but spent the dividends) became about thirteen times as wealthy as before. One hundred thousand dollars became *one million*, three hundred thousand dollars. The most affluent Americans can afford to share some of those gains, through higher taxes, in order to help people the boom left behind. This could be accomplished by some combination of eliminating unjustified deductions, more fully taxing capital gains, and imposing higher marginal tax rates on the highest levels of ordinary income.

Providing Social Insurance

Even when people are well educated and well trained, even when they have jobs at satisfactory wages, they may still suffer grievous economic hardship and be thrown into poverty if they are not protected against disasters or dislocations that can make them stop working: grave illness, a disabling accident, unemployment, old age. Only government-provided social insurance can protect everyone against these risks and against the even more devastating misfortunes that curtail their ability to learn or work in the first place. The third major strategy, therefore, is to *provide social insurance against accidents of birth or upbringing, against the major hazards of everyday life, and against the costs of retirement.* . . .

[There is a] need to defend and strengthen Social Security's retirement and disability benefits. Fortunately, despite much apocalyptic talk, the financing of the Social Security system can be bolstered relatively easily by using any of several new revenue sources—such as applying the payroll tax to high incomes as well as low, investing Trust Fund receipts in equities, and/or using general tax revenues. Individuals can also be encouraged to save more, to the benefit of the overall economy as well as themselves, by establishing universal government-subsidized savings accounts that stand outside the Social Security system and supplement rather than supplant it.

Health insurance is a more difficult issue. One reasonable approach would be to start by bolstering Medicare and Medicaid with new revenues and extending them in certain crucial ways, while relying on managed care to contain costs. (Medicare should cover prescription drugs, for example, an improvement that was beginning to be discussed at the time of this writing[1]; the reach of Medicaid could be broadened so that

1. The Medicare Prescription Drug Modernization Act, which provides prescription drug benefits to senior citizens, became law in December 2003.

it is seen as an entitlement for everyone under heavy pressure from medical bills, rather than just the poor.) A superior approach, however, which would be far cheaper, more efficient, and more just than the present system, would be to establish universal health insurance, in which all Americans are covered by a single (government) payer. The present failure of the United States to provide any health insurance at all for some forty-five million of its citizens, a failure that is unique among advanced countries, is scandalous.

Unemployment Insurance (which a Massachusetts governor once called an "economic impossibility") already helps somewhat at smoothing out the incomes of laid-off workers in cyclical industries and protects many people against the harshest effects of recessions and depressions. The main improvements needed are to raise the skimpy level of benefits and to provide for automatically extending the duration of payments during economic downturns, so that millions of unemployed workers do not run out of benefits and get condemned to destitution for reasons completely beyond their control.

But we see the concept of social insurance as going beyond these standard categories of insurance against illness, disability, retirement, and unemployment. We see it as extending also to protection from *any* loss, proceeding from *any* cause, of basic necessities like food, shelter, and medical care.

Guaranteeing the Basic Necessities of Life

Once as many Americans as possible have been helped to be physically fit, well educated, and established in well-paying jobs, the need for "safety nets"—or, better, solid floors of subsistence below which no one is allowed to fall—should be much reduced. But some people will undoubtedly still lack basic necessities. No matter how carefully education, employment, and standard social insurance programs are designed, they are likely to miss some people who need help. Yet the idea of social insurance, fully considered, suggests that *all* conceivable destitution-producing hazards should be insured against, and that we should think in terms of *right* to basic necessities of life. For this reason, the fourth major strategy is to *guarantee everyone a minimally satisfactory amount of food, shelter, medical care, and perhaps cash income.*

We are ambivalent about guaranteeing a cash income. That would not necessarily be the most efficient or effective way to help some of the people who are in greatest need. Still, the simplicity, ease of administration, and freedom-enhancing aspects of the idea make it worthy of serious consideration. The prosperity of the U.S. economy and the high level of average wages (particularly after the implementation of our other suggestions) would counteract any danger that the existence of a guaranteed minimal income would seduce many people into quitting work and living on the dole. The rewards of working and earning a much higher income, together with the self-fulfillment and social approval that working brings, would be sufficient to ensure that very few would voluntarily rely solely on the guarantee. The relatively few unfortunate people whose temporary or longer-term circumstances put them outside the reach of other programs do deserve help.

> *If we decide that minimal food, shelter, and medical care are rights to which everyone is entitled, we will be able to get rid of any damaging and unnecessary scorn, stigma, or unpleasantness associated with having to exercise those rights.*

If the American public and U.S. policy makers continue to reject the idea of a guaranteed cash income, many of the same objectives can be accomplished—perhaps somewhat more cheaply and efficiently, and with less chance of facilitating dependency on drugs or alcohol by those who are susceptible to addiction—by providing essential goods and services, rather than cash. It would not be at all difficult to design programs to do this, building, for example, on our experience with Food Stamps and rental vouchers. A *universalized* system of food coupons or credit cards *for everyone*—along with similar shelter coupons or cards good for rent and mortgage payments, and perhaps medical insurance cards as well—could efficiently and effectively guarantee the provision of these basic necessities to all Americans.

In order to make this work, the benefits should be *universal*. If we decide that minimal food, shelter, and medical care are *rights* to which everyone is entitled, we will be able to get rid of any damaging and unnecessary scorn, stigma, or unpleasantness associated with having to exercise those rights. We can distribute the benefits in equal amounts to everyone, letting millionaire CEOs as well as low-paid clerks pay restaurant and home mortgage bills in this way. Then we can tax these benefits, along with other income, on a progressive scale (that is, we can take a portion of affluent people's benefits back in taxes). That would—at a moderate administrative cost—help those in need without demeaning and expensive means tests. It should go a long way toward restoring civility, respect, and a sense of shared community among all Americans. And the cost would be only a small fraction of our roughly $85,000 in annual gross domestic product per household. . . .

Government Can Help

We believe that the chief purpose of government is to pursue policies that benefit all its citizens. All Americans should be able to enjoy what [President Abraham] Lincoln called government *for the people*. We have argued that government for the people entails, among other things, policies that greatly reduce the extent of poverty and economic inequality. And we maintain that such policies can be efficient, effective, and freedom-enhancing, rather than wasteful or freedom-reducing.

As our discussion of political reform indicates, however, a government that fully works *for* the people probably must also be government *by* the people. Only citizens themselves can be trusted, in the long run, to favor and push for the polities that would benefit them most. The democratic ideal implies that each citizen should have equal political power, an equal political voice. Unless this ideal of equal political power is realized in fact, unless the disproportionate influence of corporations, the affluent, and well-organized special interests is curtailed, it will be extremely difficult to deal effectively with the problems of poverty and inequality.

2

Government Programs Do Not Help America's Poor

Myron Magnet

Myron Magnet is the editor of City Journal, *the Manhattan Institute's quarterly magazine of urban affairs, and a former member of the board of editors of* Fortune *magazine. He is the author of five books, including* Dickens and the Social Order.

Government welfare programs have created an inter-generational class of permanently poor people who engage in self-destructive behaviors because the government is there to bail them out. The failure of welfare programs in America and Europe shows that encouraging dependency is not helpful to the poor. Rather, the poor need more opportunities to work and succeed. For those who are unable to do so, it would be better to give money to private faith-based charities to help them rather than to rely on government programs.

W hat ever happened to compassionate conservatism? Despite the Bush administration's focus on the war against terror, the idea didn't disappear. But as White House thinking developed, it got incorporated into a larger, more profound domestic theory. Yes, we need a safety net, the current view seems to go; but we don't need a Europe-style welfare state. What's called for is the traditional American "opportunity society," as much a boon to the poor as to everyone else.

Implicit in compassionate conservatism was the epochal paradigm shift that is now all but explicit. Taken together, compassionate conservatism's elements added up to a sweeping rejection of liberal orthodoxy about how to help the poor, which a half century's worth of experience had discredited. If you want to help the poor, compassionate conservatives argued, liberate them from dependency through welfare reform; free their communities from criminal anarchy through activist policing; give them the education they need to succeed in a modern economy by holding their schools accountable; and let them enjoy the rewards of work by taxing their modest wages lightly—or not at all.

For the worst-off—those hampered by addiction or alcohol or faulty socialization—let the government pay private organizations, especially religious ones, to help. Such people need a change of heart to solve their problems, the president himself deeply believed; and while a clergyman or a therapist might help them, a bureaucrat couldn't.

In fact a welfare-department worker might do harm even beyond providing money to fuel self-destructive behavior. Rather than understand that an inner transformation is what such a person needs, the welfare worker might well try to persuade him that his plight stems from an unjust economy, which provides him insufficient opportunity, or even purposely keeps a fraction of the population unemployed, so as to hold down the wages of those who are working. His problem thus is the result of vast, impersonal forces, of which he is the victim (and doubly the victim if he is black in *racist* America). In other words, capitalism is inherently defective and unjust, and therefore we need a welfare state to mitigate its harshness.

Conservative Impatience

President [George W.] Bush entered the White House with no patience for such a view. What he understood was that the War on Poverty—an array of [Lyndon B. Johnson] era legislation that boosted welfare benefits and established other programs for the poor, including Medicaid—created its own form of depression, as women long dependent on welfare became so convinced of their own inferiority that they could hardly present themselves without trembling at a job interview. And, as a far worse psychological consequence, the sense of victimization and of entitlement to government support that the War on Poverty fostered created a corrosive self-pity and resentment among the children of its beneficiaries, and their children's children. The self-pity led to drink and drugs; the resentment to crime and violence; and both together to a perpetuation of irresponsibility, dysfunction, and failure over the generations. The first-line antidote, in Mr. Bush's view, would be the intervention of a counselor, preferably faith-based.

> *Taken together, compassionate conservatism's elements added up to a sweeping rejection of liberal orthodoxy about how to help the poor, which a half century's worth of experience had discredited.*

But if there was a permanent class of poor, the cause was not a failure of capitalism but of the War on Poverty, which reinforced such self-defeating attitudes. Clearly, as the administration understood, American capitalism was a dynamo of job creation and opportunity. President Bush's generation, after all, had seen the astonishing restructuring of U.S. industry in the 1980s, when, in response to foreign competition, companies slimmed down, boosted productivity and quality, and kept their markets and prosperity; while their laid-off workers didn't permanently succumb to paralyzing depression but instead found—or created—new jobs.

Moreover, as a Texan, Mr. Bush had seen waves of Mexican immigrants flooding in to take jobs no one previously knew existed—still more evidence that there was no crisis of opportunity—while in the cities, a new wave of immigrant-run greengroceries, nail salons, construction firms, even commercial fish farms in Bronx basements, gave the lie to the failure-of-capitalism theory.

And, on top of all that, the overwhelming success of the 1996 Welfare Reform Act, which became ever clearer during President Bush's first term, utterly exploded the idea that the hard-core poor were not working because of a lack of jobs. Welfare mothers crowded into the work force; the rolls dropped by roughly half. Not only were their children not freezing to death on the streets by the thousands, as even so wise an observer as the late Sen. Patrick Moynihan had predicted they would, but in fact child poverty reached its lowest point ever three years after welfare reform. Lack of opportunity? Hardly.

A False Premise

The War on Poverty rests on a false premise: that capitalism creates a permanent class of poor. And War on Poverty attitudes have a deeply harmful effect on those entrammeled in America's current welfare state. So the second Bush term is bringing the War on Poverty—demonstrably a cataclysmic mistake—to an end. A glance at the administration's [2005] budget shows the ongoing dismantling of antipoverty programs: a sharp reduction in the Community Development Block Grant, the main conduit for funneling federal money to cities; the reduction in [the Department of Housing and Urban Development] money for Section 8 subsidized housing vouchers, which abets the formation of dysfunctional single-parent families and destabilizes respectable working-class neighborhoods; and the shrinkage of ever-expanding Medicaid. Welfare is now temporary assistance in adversity, not a permanent way of life; and we can expect welfare reform's conditions to become even stricter when the 1996 Act finally gets reauthorized.

> *A welfare-department worker might do harm even beyond providing money to fuel self-destructive behavior.*

Supporters of the old paradigm are naturally apoplectic over such a transformation; and their outrage reveals just how sweeping a welfare state they really champion. As Georgetown law professor Peter Edelman, who resigned from the Clinton administration to protest the president's signing of the 1996 welfare reform, told columnist William Raspberry: "For virtually all of my adulthood, America has had a bipartisan agreement that we ought to provide some basic framework of programs and policies that provide a safety net, not just for the poor but for a large portion of the American people who need help to manage." How large a portion? Well, figures Mr. Raspberry, "the lower third of the economy." Think about that: nearly 100 million Americans as clients of the federal government. This is not temporary assistance but a European-style "social-democratic" (that is, socialist) welfare state. It is the political culture of America's old cities, with their hordes of government-supported clients, employees, and retirees—a culture that has produced slow or negative job and population growth. And this is exactly what the Bush administration does not want.

European Failure Versus American Opportunity

The failure of the European model, explicitly based on the belief that free-market capitalism is dangerous and needs to be tied down with a thousand trammels . . . is one of the signal facts of our era, along with the failure of communism. In Europe, the idea that capitalism creates a permanently jobless class has become a self-fulfilling prophecy, as strict regulation and the high taxes needed to pay lavish welfare and unemployment benefits have resulted in half the U.S. rate of job creation, twice the rate of unemployment, and thus little opportunity.

Meanwhile retirees, often young and vigorous, go off for government-funded visits to health spas at taxpayer expense. Even if this were morally sustainable, it is not economically so. . . . But with so many voters on the dole, or employed by the government to administer the vast welfare-state apparatus, who knows whether reform or collapse will occur first?

[President Bush's view] is part of the large and coherent world view that has evolved out of compassionate conservatism. What has always made America exceptional is limitless opportunity for everyone, at all levels—the ability to find a job, to advance up the ladder as you prove yourself, and to prosper. The poor especially have flocked to these shores for just this chance, and have proved the promise true. A giant welfare state—whether its clients are the poor, the "lower third of the economy," or a cohort of government-pensioned retirees who almost outnumber the taxpaying workers who support them— hampers the job creation that makes all this opportunity possible. President Bush is determined to keep the dynamism vibrant, and to encourage and empower the poor to take part in it, rather than to suggest they are unequal to the task.

The Europeans call this "cowboy capitalism." If so, then yee-haw!

3

Promoting Marriage Will Reduce Poverty in America

Robert E. Rector and Melissa G. Pardue

Robert E. Rector is a senior research fellow in domestic policy studies at the Heritage Foundation, a research and educational institute whose mission is to formulate and promote conservative public policies. Melissa G. Pardue is a policy analyst in the Department of Domestic Policy Studies at the Heritage Foundation.

Marriage provides many benefits to society, including keeping children out of poverty. Children born outside of wedlock are much more likely to live in poverty than those who are not, and most welfare benefits are paid to single parent families. President George W. Bush has proposed the Healthy Marriage Initiative to promote marriage through education programs targeted at unmarried couples and at-risk high school students. The Healthy Marriage Initiative will benefit low-income single women and their children.

Editor's Note: The Healthy Marriage Initiative had not been passed into law as of April 2005.

The erosion of marriage during the past four decades has had large-scale negative effects on both children and adults: It lies at the heart of many of the social problems with which the government currently grapples. The beneficial effects of marriage on individuals and society are beyond reasonable dispute, and there is a broad and growing consensus that government policy should promote rather than discourage healthy marriage.

In response to these trends, President George W. Bush has proposed . . . the creation of a pilot program to promote healthy and stable marriage.[1] Participation in the program would be strictly voluntary. . . .

Today, nearly one-third of all American children are born outside marriage. That's one out-of-wedlock birth every 35 seconds. Of those born inside marriage, a great many children will experience their parents' divorce before they reach age 18. More than half of the children in the United States will spend all or part of their childhood in never-formed or broken families.

The collapse of marriage is the principal cause of child poverty in the United States. Children raised by never-married mothers are seven times more likely to live in poverty than children raised by their biological parents in intact marriages. Overall, approximately 80 percent of long-term child poverty in the United States occurs among children from broken or never-formed families.

It is often argued that strengthening marriage would have little impact on child poverty because absent fathers earn too little. This is not true: The typical non-married father earns $17,500 per year at the time his child is born. Some 70 percent of poor single mothers would be lifted out of poverty if they were married to their children's father. . . . If the mothers remain single and do not marry the fathers of their children, some 55 percent will be poor. However, if the mothers married the fathers, the poverty rate would drop to 17 percent. . . .

The Welfare System

The growth of single-parent families has had an enormous impact on government. The welfare system for children is overwhelming a subsidy system for single-parent families. Some three-quarters of the aid to children—given through programs such as food stamps, Medicaid, public housing, Temporary Assistance to Needy Families (TANF), and the Earned Income Tax Credit—goes to single-parent families. . . .

Despite the overwhelming evidence of the benefits of mar-

1. Although President Bush has proposed the Healthy Marriage Initiative several times, it has not been passed into law as of April 2005.

riage to families and society, the sad fact is that, for more than four decades, the welfare system has penalized and discouraged marriage. The U.S. welfare system is currently composed of more than 70 means-tested aid programs providing cash, food, housing, medical care, and social services to low-income persons. Each year, over $200 billion flows through its system to families with children. While it is widely accepted that the welfare system is biased against marriage, relatively few understand how this bias operates. Many erroneously believe that welfare programs have eligibility criteria that directly exclude marriage couples. This is not true.

> *The collapse of marriage is the principal cause of child poverty in the United States.*

Nevertheless, welfare programs do penalize marriage and reward single parenthood because of the inherent design of all means-tested programs. In a means-tested program, benefits are reduced as non-welfare income rises. Thus, under any means-tested system, a mother will receive greater benefits if she remains single than she would if she were married to a working husband. Welfare not only serves as a substitute for a husband, but it actually penalizes marriage because a low-income couple will experience a significant drop in combined income if they marry. . . .

Promoting Marriage

In recognition of the widespread benefits of marriage to individuals and society, the federal welfare reform legislation enacted in 1996 set forth clear goals: to increase the number of two-parent families and to reduce out-of-wedlock childbearing. Regrettably, in the years since this reform, most states have done very little to advance these objectives directly. Out of more than $100 billion in federal TANF funds disbursed over the past seven years, only about $20 million—a miniscule 0.02 percent—has been spent on promoting marriage.

Recognizing this shortcoming, President Bush has sought to meet the original goals of welfare reform by proposing a new model program to promote healthy marriage. . . . The proposed program would seek to increase healthy marriage by providing individuals and couples with:

- Accurate information on the value of marriage in the lives of men, women, and children;
- Marriage-skills education that will enable couples to reduce conflict and increase the happiness and longevity of their relationship; and
- Experimental reductions in the financial penalties against marriage that are currently contained in all federal welfare programs.

All participation in the President's marriage program would be voluntary. The initiative would utilize existing marriage-skills education programs that have proven effective in decreasing conflict and increasing happiness and stability among couples. These programs have also been shown to be effective in reducing domestic violence. The pro-marriage initiative would not merely seek to increase marriage rates among target couples, but also would provide ongoing support to help at-risk couples maintain healthy marriages over time.

> *A well-designed marriage initiative would target women and men earlier in their lives when attitudes and relationships were initially being formed.*

The plan would not create government bureaucracies to provide marriage training. Instead, the government would contract with private organizations that have successful track records in providing marriage-skills education.

Prevention Instead of Repair

The President's Healthy Marriage Initiative is often characterized as seeking to increase marriage among welfare (TANF) recipients. This is somewhat inaccurate. Most welfare mothers have poor relationships with their children's father. In many cases, the relationship disintegrated long ago. Attempting to promote healthy marriage in these situations is a bit like trying to glue Humpty-Dumpty together after he has fallen off the wall. By contrast, a well-designed marriage initiative would tar-

get women and men earlier in their lives when attitudes and relationships were initially being formed. It would also seek to
strengthen existing marriages to reduce divorce.

> **"** *To any objective observer, the link between the
> erosion of marriage and high levels of child poverty
> and welfare dependence was obvious.* **"**

Typically, marriage promotion programs would provide information about the long-term value of marriage to at-risk
high school students. They would teach relationship skills to
unmarried couples before the woman became pregnant with a
focus on preventing pregnancy before a couple has made a
commitment to healthy marriage. Marriage programs would
also provide marriage and relationship education to unmarried couples at the "magic moment" of a child's birth and offer marriage-skills training to low-income married couples to
improve marriage quality and reduce the likelihood of divorce.

The primary focus of marriage programs would be preven-
tative—not reparative. The programs would seek to prevent the
isolation and poverty of welfare mothers by intervening at an
early point before a pattern of broken relationships and welfare
dependence had emerged. By fostering better life decisions and
stronger relationships skills, marriage programs can increase
child well-being and adult happiness, and reduce child poverty
and welfare dependence. . . .

Societal Change

More than 40 years ago, Senator Daniel Patrick Moynihan—at
that time, a member of President Lyndon Johnson's White
House staff—wrote poignantly of the social ills stemming from
the decline of marriage in the black community. Since that
time, the dramatic erosion of marriage has afflicted the white
community as well. Today, the social and economic ills fostered by marital collapse have exceeded Senator Moynihan's
worst expectations.

Tragically, when Senator Moynihan's prescient report on
marriage and the family was released in the early 1960s, it was
met with a firestorm of abuse. So vitriolic was the attack against

Moynihan that a virtual wall of silence came to surround the issues he raised. For 30 years, nearly all public discussion about the importance of marriage, and the role that government policy played in either supporting or undermining it, was muffled. Meanwhile, marriage declined and out-of-wedlock childbearing soared. When Moynihan wrote his report in the early 1960s, 7 percent of all American children were born out of wedlock: Today, the number is 33 percent. To any objective observer, the link between the erosion of marriage and high levels of child poverty and welfare dependence was obvious, but for decades, this topic was scrupulously avoided in public discussion.

In the early 1990s, the wall of silence surrounding the marriage issue began to crumble. In his 1993 State of the Union address, President Bill Clinton spoke forcefully of the harm wrought by the decline of marriage in America. His remarks echoed those of Moynihan 30 years earlier. By the late 1990s, most responsible individuals, on both the left and the right, had acknowledged the importance of marriage to the well-being of children, adults, and society. Most affirmed the need for government policies to strengthen marriage.

In response, President Bush has developed the Healthy Marriage Initiative: the first positive step toward strengthening the institution of marriage since the Moynihan report four decades ago. The proposal represents a strategy to increase healthy marriage—carefully crafted on the basis of all existing research on the topic of promoting and strengthening marriage.

Looking Forward

The President's Healthy Marriage Initiative is a future-oriented, preventive policy. It will foster better life-planning skills—encouraging couples to develop loving, committed marriages before bringing children into the world, as opposed to having children before trust and commitment between the parents has been established. The marriage program will encourage couples to re-examine and improve their relationships and plan wisely for the future, rather than stumbling blindly into a childbirth for which neither parent may be prepared. The program will also provide marriage-skills education to married couples to improve their relationships and to reduce the probability of divorce.

Ideally, pro-marriage interventions for non-married couples would occur well before the conception of a child. A second—less desirable, but still fruitful—point of intervention would be at the time of a child's birth: a time when the majority of unmarried couples express an active interest in marriage. By providing young couples with the tools needed to build healthy, stable marriages, the Marriage Initiative would substantially reduce future rates of welfare dependence, child poverty, domestic violence, and other social ills.

There is now broad bipartisan recognition that healthy marriage is a natural protective institution that, in most cases, promotes the well-being of men, women, and children: It is the foundation of a healthy society. Yet, for decades, government policy has remained indifferent or hostile to marriage. Government programs sought merely to pick up the pieces as marriages failed or—worse—actively undermined marriage.

President Bush seeks to change this policy of indifference and hostility. There is no group that will gain more from this change than low-income single women, most of whom hope for a happy, healthy marriage in their future. President Bush seeks to provide young couples with the knowledge and skills to accomplish their dreams. The Senate would be wise to affirm their support for marriage by passing welfare reform reauthorization and enacting the President's Healthy Marriage Initiative.

4

Promoting Marriage Will Not Reduce Poverty in America

Katha Pollitt

Katha Pollitt is a columnist for the Nation *magazine. She has written for a variety of publications and has appeared on a number of television and radio programs.*

Conservatives have tried a number of ways to increase marriage rates among welfare recipients, including offering monthly bonuses for those who get married. These measures have failed, but right-wing ideologues still want to force welfare recipients to participate in programs that encourage marriage. Not only will these efforts not increase the marriage rates among welfare recipients, they may also be harmful because they would push poor women into marriages with abusive men. There is also no guarantee that marriage would lift a single mother out of poverty; research shows that 30 percent of poor single fathers are unemployed and 40 percent have been incarcerated.

W hat would the government have to do to convince you to get married when you otherwise wouldn't? More than pay you $80 a month, I'll bet, the amount Wisconsin's much-ballyhooed "Bridefare" pilot program offered unwed teen welfare mothers beginning in the early nineties, which is perhaps why then-Governor Tommy Thompson, now Health and Human Services Secretary, was uninterested in having it properly evaluated and why you don't hear much about Bridefare today. OK, how abut $100 a month? That's what West Virginia is currently offering to add a couple's welfare benefits if they wed. But even though the state has simultaneously cut by 25 percent the checks of recipients living with adults to whom they are not married (including, in some cases, their own grown children, if you can believe that!), results have been modest: Only around 1,600 couples have applied for the bonus and presumably some of these would have married anyway. With the state's welfare budget expected to show a $90 million shortfall by 2003, the marriage bonus is likely to be quietly abolished.

> ❝ Since the stick of work and the carrot of cash have both proved ineffective in herding women to the altar, family values conservatives are calling for more lectures. ❞

Although welfare reform was sold to the public as promoting work, the Personal Responsibility and Work Opportunity Reconciliation Act of 1996 actually opens with the declaration that "marriages is the foundation of a successful society." According to Charles Murray, Robert Rector and other right-wing ideologues, welfare enabled poor women to rely on the state instead of husbands; forcing them off the dole and into the rigors of low-wage employment would push them into marriage, restore "the family" and lift children out of poverty. That was always a silly idea. For one thing, as any single woman could have told them, it wrongly assumed that whether a woman married was only up to her, for another, it has been well documented that the men available to poor women are also poor and often (like the women) have other problems as well: In one study, 30 percent of poor single fathers were unemployed in the week before the survey and almost 40 percent had been incarcerated; drugs, drink, violence, poor health and bad attitudes were not uncommon. Would Murray want *his* daughter to marry a guy with even one of those strikes against him? Not surprisingly, there has been no upsurge of marriage among former welfare recipients since 1996. Of all births, the proportion that are to unwed mothers has stayed roughly where it was, at 33 percent.

Lectures on Marriage

Since the stick of work and the carrot of cash have both proved ineffective in herding women to the altar, family values conservatives are calling for more lectures. Marriage promotion will be a hot item when welfare reform comes up for reauthorization later this year [2002]. At the federal level conservatives are calling for 10 percent of all TANF [Temporary Assistance to Needy Families] money to be set aside for promoting marriage[1]; Utah, Arizona and Oklahoma have already raided TANF to fund such ventures as a "healthy marriage" handbook for couples seeking a marriage license. And it's not just Republicans: Senator Joe Lieberman and Representative Ben Cardin, the ranking Democrat on the House Ways and Means Committee, are also interested in funding "family formation." In place of cash bonuses to individuals, which at least put money in the pockets of poor people, look for massive funding of faith-based marriage preparation courses (and never you mind that pesky separation of church and state), for fatherhood intervention programs, classes to instruct poor single moms in the benefits of marriage (as if they didn't know!), for self-help groups like Marriage Savers, abstinence education for kids and grownups alike and, of course, ingenious pilot projects by the dozen. There's even been a proposal to endow pro-marriage professorships at state universities—and don't forget millions of dollars for evaluation, follow-up, filing and forgetting.

> *Remember when it was conservatives who argued against social engineering and micromanaging people's lives and 'throwing money at the problem'?*

There's nothing wrong with programs that aim to raise people's marital IQ—I love that journalistic evergreen about the engaged couple who take a quiz in order to qualify for a church wedding and call if off when they discover he wants seven kids

1. Although President Bush has proposed the Healthy Marriage Initiative several times, it has not become law as of April 2005. He has also proposed that states could receive matching grants if they spend funds from the Temporary Assistance to Needy Families on programs that promote healthy marriages.

38

and she wants to live in a tree. But remember when it was conservatives who argued against social engineering and micromanaging people's private lives and "throwing money at the problem"?

Potential Harm

Domestic violence experts have warned that poor women may find themselves pushed into marrying their abusers and staying with them—in a disturbing bit of Senate testimony, Mike McManus of Marriage Savers said domestic violence could usually be overcome with faith-based help. Is that the message women in danger should be getting? But there are even larger issues: Marriage is a deeply personal, intimate matter, involving our most private, barely articulated selves. Why should the government try to maneuver reluctant women into dubious choices just because they are poor? Even as a meal ticket wedlock is no panacea—that marriage is a cure for poverty is only true if you marry someone who isn't poor, who will share his income with you and your children, who won't divorce you later and leave you worse off than ever. The relation between poverty and marriage is virtually the opposite of what pro-marriage ideologues claim: It isn't that getting married gives feckless poor people middle-class values and stability, it's that stable middle-class people are the ones who can "afford" to be married. However marriage functioned a half-century ago, today it is a class marker. Instead of marketing marriage as a poverty program, how much better to invest in poor women—and poor men—as human beings in their own right: with education, training for high-paying jobs, housing, mental health services, really good childcare for their kids. Every TANF dollar spent on marital propaganda means a dollar less for programs that really help people.

The very fact that welfare reformers are reduced to bribing cajoling and guilt-tripping people into marriage should tell us something. Or have they just not hit on the right incentive?

5

Raising Wages for Low-Wage Workers Will Help America's Poor

Barbara Ehrenreich

Barbara Ehrenreich is the author of several books, including
Blood Rites: The Worst Years of Our Lives, Fear of Falling,
and Nickel and Dimed: On (Not) Getting By in America,
from which the following viewpoint was excerpted. She is a
frequent contributor to magazines such as Time, Harper's,
and New Republic.

The wages of the poor have risen very slowly when compared with those of other classes. One reason for this is
that employers of low-wage workers are reluctant to
raise wages. Another reason is that low-wage workers
have a hard time moving to jobs that might pay them
more because of transportation problems. Also, they do
not have information about other opportunities that
might be available in the job market. Furthermore, there
is a "money taboo" encouraged by employers, in which
people are afraid to disclose their salaries and therefore
do not realize how underpaid they are. America would
be better off if the working poor received higher wages.

E very city where I worked in the course of this project[1] was
experiencing what local businesspeople define as a "labor
shortage"—commented on in the local press and revealed by the

1. The author spent a period of time working low-wage jobs in different locations
and wrote a book about her experiences.

40

ubiquitous signs saying "Now Hiring" or, more imperiously, "We Are Now Accepting Applications." Yet wages for people near the bottom of the labor market remain fairly flat, even "stagnant." . . . Federal Reserve chief Alan Greenspan, who spends much of his time anxiously scanning the horizon for the slightest hint of such "inflationary" gains, was pleased to inform Congress in July 2000 that the forecast seemed largely trouble-free. He went so far as to suggest that the economic laws linking low unemployment to wage increases may no longer be operative, which is a little like saying that the law of supply and demand has been repealed. Some economists argue that the apparent paradox rests on an illusion: there is no real "labor shortage," only a shortage of people willing to work at the wages currently being offered. You might as well talk about a "Lexus shortage"—which there is, in a sense, for anyone unwilling to pay $40,000 for a car.

> *Employers resist wage increases with every trick they can think of and every ounce of strength they can summon.*

In fact, wages *have* risen, or did rise, anyway, between 1996 and 1999. When I called around to various economists in the summer of 2000 and complained about the inadequacy of the wages available to entry-level workers, this was their first response: "But wages are going up!" According to the Economic Policy Institute, the poorest 10 percent of American workers saw their wages rise from $5.49 an hour (in 1999 dollars) in 1996 to $6.05 in 1999. Moving up the socioeconomic ladder, the next 10 percent–sized slice of Americans—which is roughly where I found myself as a low-wage worker—went from $6.80 an hour in 1996 to $7.35 in 1999.

Obviously we have one of those debates over whether the glass is half empty or half full; the increases that seem to have mollified many economists do not seem so impressive to me. To put the wage gains of the past four years in somewhat dismal perspective: they have not been sufficient to bring low-wage workers up to the amounts they were earning twenty-seven years ago, in 1973. In the first quarter of 2000, the poorest 10 percent of workers were earning only 91 percent of what they earned in the distant era of Watergate and disco music. Furthermore, of all workers, the poorest have made the least progress back to their 1973 wage levels. Relatively well-off workers in the eighth decile, or 10 percent–sized slice, where earnings are about $20 an hour, are now making 106.6 percent of what they earned in 1973. When I persisted in my carping to the economists, they generally backed down a bit, conceding that while wages at the bottom are going up, they're not going up very briskly. Lawrence Michel at the Economic Policy Institute . . . heightened the mystery when he observed that productivity—to which wages are theoretically tied—has been rising at such a healthy clip that "workers should be getting much more."

Keeping Wages Down

The most obvious reason why they're not is that employers resist wage increases with every trick they can think of and every ounce of strength they can summon. I had an opportunity to query one of my own employers on this subject in Maine. . . . Ted, my boss at The Maids, drove me about forty minutes to a house where I was needed to reinforce a shorthanded team. In the course of complaining about his hard lot in life, he avowed that he could double his business overnight if only he could find enough reliable workers. As politely as possible, I asked him why he didn't just raise the pay. The question seemed to slide right off him. We offer "mothers' hours," he told me, meaning that the workday was supposedly over at three—as if to say, "With a benefit like that, how could anybody complain about wages?"

> *Many employers will offer almost anything— free meals, subsidized transportation, store discounts—rather than raise wages.*

In fact, I suspect that the free breakfast he provided us represented the only concession to the labor shortage that he was prepared to make. Similarly, the Wal-Mart where I worked was offering free doughnuts once a week to any employees who could arrange to take their breaks while the supply lasted. As Louis Uchitelle has reported in the *New York Times*, many employers will offer almost anything—free meals, subsidized transportation, store discounts—rather than raise wages. The reason for this, in the words of one employer, is that such extras "can be shed more easily" than wage increases when changes in the market seem to make them unnecessary. In the same spirit, automobile manufacturers would rather offer their customers cash rebates than reduced prices; the advantage of the rebate is that it seems like a gift and can be withdrawn without explanation.

Why Do Workers Put Up with It?

But the resistance of employers only raises a second and ultimately more intractable question: Why isn't this resistance met by more effective counterpressure from the workers themselves? In evading and warding off wage increases, employers are of course behaving in an economically rational fashion; their business isn't to make their employees more comfortable and secure but to maximize the bottom line. So why don't employees behave in an equally rational fashion, demanding higher wages of their employers or seeking out better-paying jobs? The assumption behind the law of supply and demand, as it applies to labor, is that workers will sort themselves out as effectively as marbles on an inclined plane—gravitating to the better-paying jobs and either leaving the recalcitrant employers behind or forcing them to up the pay. "Economic man," that great abstraction of economic science, is supposed to do whatever it takes, within certain limits, to maximize his economic advantage.

I was baffled, initially, by what seemed like a certain lack of get-up-and-go on the part of my fellow workers. Why didn't they just leave for a better-paying job, as I did when I moved from the Hearthside to Jerry's? Part of the answer is that actual humans experience a little more "friction" than marbles do, and the poorer they are, the more constrained their mobility usually is. Low-wage people who don't have cars are often dependent on a relative who is willing to drop them off and pick them up again each day, sometimes on a route that includes the babysitter's house or the child care center. Change your place of work and you may be confronted with an impossible topographical problem to solve, or at least a reluctant driver to persuade. Some of my coworkers, in Minneapolis as well as Key West, rode bikes to work, and this clearly limited their geographical range. For those who do possess cars, there is still the problem of gas prices, not to mention the general hassle, which is of course far more onerous for the carless, of getting around to fill out applications, to be interviewed, to take drug tests. I have mentioned, too, the general reluctance to exchange the devil you know for one that you don't know, even when the latter is tempting you with a better wage-benefit package. At each new job, you have to start all over, clueless and friendless.

A Lack of Information

There is another way that low-income workers differ from "economic man." For the laws of economics to work, the "players" need to be well informed about their options. The ideal case—and I've read that the technology for this is just around the corner—would be the consumer whose Palm Pilot displays the menu and prices for every restaurant or store he or she passes. Even without such technological assistance, affluent job hunters expect to study the salary-benefit packages offered by their potential employers, watch the financial news to find out if these packages are in line with those being offered in other regions or fields, and probably do a little bargaining before taking a job.

> *For the laws of economics to work, the 'players' need to be well informed about their options.*

But there are no Palm Pilots, cable channels, or Web sites to advise the low-wage job seeker. She has only the help-wanted signs and the want ads to go on, and most of these coyly refrain from mentioning numbers. So information about who earns what and where has to travel by word of mouth, and for inexplicable cultural reasons, this is a very slow and unreliable route. Twin Cities job market analyst Kristine Jacobs pinpoints what she calls the "money taboo" as a major factor preventing workers from optimizing their earnings. "There's a code of silence surrounding issues related to individuals' earnings," she told me. "We confess everything else in our society—sex, crime, illness. But no one wants to reveal what they earn or how they got it. The money taboo is the one thing that employers can always count on." I suspect that this "taboo" operates most effectively among the lowest-paid people, because, in a society that endlessly celebrates its dot-com billionaires and centimillionaire athletes, $7 or even $10 an hour can feel like a mark of innate inferiority. So you may or may not find out that, say, the Target down the road is paying better than Wal-Mart, even if you have a sister-in-law working there.

> *There seems to be a vicious cycle at work here, making ours not just an economy but a culture of extreme inequality.*

Employers, of course, do little to encourage the economic literacy of their workers. They may exhort potential customers to "Compare Our Prices!" but they're not eager to have workers do the same with wages. I have mentioned the way the hiring process seems designed, in some cases, to prevent any discussion or even disclosure of wages—whisking the applicant from interview to orientation before the crass subject of money can be raised. Some employers go further; instead of relying on the informal "money taboo" to keep workers from discussing and comparing wages, they specifically enjoin workers from doing so. . . .

A Dictatorial Workplace

So if low-wage workers do not always behave in an economically rational way, that is, as free agents within a capitalist democracy, it is because they dwell in a place that is neither free nor in any way democratic. When you enter the low-wage workplace—and many of the medium-wage workplaces as well—you check your civil liberties at the door, leave America and all it supposedly stands for behind, and learn to zip your lips for the duration of the shift. The consequences of this routine surrender go beyond the issues of wages and poverty. We can hardly pride ourselves on being the world's preeminent democracy, after all, if large numbers of citizens spend half their waking hours in what amounts, in plain terms, to a dictatorship.

Any dictatorship takes a psychological toll on its subjects. If you are treated as an untrustworthy person—a potential slacker, drug addict, or thief—you may begin to feel less trust-worthy yourself. If you are constantly reminded of your lowly position in the social hierarchy, whether by individual man-agers or by a plethora of impersonal rules, you begin to accept that unfortunate status. To draw for a moment from an entirely different corner of my life, that part of me still attached to the biological sciences, there is ample evidence that animals—rats and monkeys, for example—that are forced into a subordinate status within their social systems adapt their brain chemistry accordingly, becoming "depressed" in humanlike ways. Their behavior is anxious and withdrawn; the level of serotonin (the neurotransmitter boosted by some antidepressants) declines in their brains. And—what is especially relevant here—they avoid fighting even in self-defense.

> **❝** Guilt doesn't go anywhere near far enough; the appropriate emotion is shame—shame at our own dependency, in this case, on the underpaid labor of others. **❞**

Humans are, of course, vastly more complicated; even in sit-uations of extreme subordination, we can pump up our self-esteem with thoughts of our families, our religion, our hopes for the future. But as much as any other social animal, and more so than many, we depend for our self-image on the humans imme-diately around us—to the point of altering our perceptions of the world so as to fit in with theirs. My guess is that the indignities imposed on so many low-wage workers—the drug tests, the con-stant surveillance, being "reamed out" by managers—are part of what keeps wages low. If you're made to feel unworthy enough, you may come to think that what you're paid is what you are ac-tually worth.

It is hard to imagine any other function for workplace au-thoritarianism. Managers may truly believe that, without their unremitting efforts, all work would quickly grind to a halt. That is not my impression. While I encountered some cynics and plenty of people who had learned to budget their energy, I never met an actual slacker or, for that matter, a drug addict or thief. On the contrary, I was amazed and sometimes saddened by the pride people took in jobs that rewarded them so meagerly, either in wages or in recognition. Often, in fact, these people experienced management as an obstacle to getting the job done as it should be done. Waitresses chafed at managers' stinginess toward the customers; housecleaners resented the time constraints that sometimes made them cut corners; retail workers wanted the floor to be beautiful, not cluttered with excess stock as management required. Left to themselves, they devised systems of cooperation and work sharing; when there was a crisis, they rose to it. In fact, it was often hard to see what the function of management was, other than to exact obeisance.

There seems to be a vicious cycle at work here, making ours not just an economy but a culture of extreme inequality. Corporate decision makers, and even some two-bit entrepreneurs like my boss at The Maids, occupy an economic position miles above that of the underpaid people whose labor they depend on. For reasons that have more to do with class—and often racial—prejudice than with actual experience, they tend to fear and distrust the category of people from which they recruit their workers. Hence the perceived need for repressive management and intrusive measures like drug and personality testing. But these things cost money—$20,000 or more a year for a manager, $100 a pop for a drug test, and so on—and the high cost of repression results in ever more pressure to hold wages down. The larger society seems to be caught up in a similar cycle: cutting public services for the poor, which are sometimes referred to collectively as the "social wage," while investing ever more heavily in prisons and cops. And in the larger society, too, the cost of repression becomes another factor weighing against the expansion or restoration of needed services. It is a tragic cycle, condemning us to ever deeper inequality, and in the long run, almost no one benefits but the agents of repression themselves. . . .

Employed in Poverty

Americans of the newspaper-reading professional middle class are used to thinking of poverty as a consequence of unemployment. During the heyday of downsizing in the Reagan years, it very often was, and it still is for many inner-city residents who have no way of getting to the proliferating entry-level jobs on urban peripheries. When unemployment causes poverty, we know how to state the problem—typically, "the economy isn't growing fast enough"—and we know what the traditional liberal solution is—"full employment." But when we have full or nearly full employment, when jobs are available to any job seeker who can get to them, then the problem goes deeper and begins to cut into that web of expectations that make up the "social contract." According to a . . . poll conducted by Jobs for the Future, a Boston-based employment research firm, 94 percent of Americans agree that "people who work fulltime should be able to earn enough to keep their families out of poverty." I grew up hearing over and over, to the point of tedium, that "hard work" was the secret of success: "Work hard and you'll get ahead" or "It's hard work that got us where we are." No one ever said that you could work hard— harder even than you ever thought possible—and still find yourself sinking ever deeper into poverty and debt.

> **To be a member of the working poor is to be an anonymous donor, a nameless benefactor, to everyone else.**

When poor single mothers had the option of remaining out of the labor force on welfare, the middle and upper middle class tended to view them with a certain impatience, if not disgust. The welfare poor were excoriated for their laziness, their persistence in reproducing in unfavorable circumstances, their presumed addictions, and above all for their "dependency." Here they were, content to live off "government handouts" instead of seeking "self-sufficiency," like everyone else, through a job. They needed to get their act together, learn how to wind an alarm clock, get out there and get to work. But now that government has largely withdrawn its "handouts," now that the overwhelming majority of the poor are out there toiling in Wal-Mart or Wendy's—well, what are we to think of them? Disapproval and condescension no longer apply, so what outlook makes sense?

Guilt, you may be thinking warily. Isn't that what we're supposed to feel? But guilt doesn't go anywhere near far enough; the appropriate emotion is shame—shame at our *own* dependency, in this case, on the underpaid labor of others. When someone works for less pay than she can live on—when, for example, she goes hungry so that you can eat more cheaply and conveniently—then she has made a great sacrifice for you, she has made you a gift of some part of her abilities, her health, and her life. The "working poor," as they are approvingly termed, are in fact the major philanthropists of our society. They neglect their own children so that the children of others will be cared for; they live in substandard housing so that other homes will be shiny and perfect; they endure privation so that inflation will be low and stock prices high. To be a member of the working poor is to be an anonymous donor, a nameless benefactor, to everyone else. As Gail, one of my restaurant coworkers put it, "you give and you give."

Someday, of course—and I will make no predictions as to exactly when—they are bound to tire of getting so little in return and to demand to be paid what they're worth. There'll be a lot of anger when that day comes, and strikes and disruption. But the sky will not fall, and we will all be better off for it in the end.

6

The United States Should Not Pass Living-Wage Laws

Carl F. Horowitz

Carl F. Horowitz is a Washington, D.C.–area consultant on labor, welfare reform, immigration, and other policy issues, and a former policy analyst at the Heritage Foundation, a research and educational institute whose mission is to formulate and promote conservative public policies.

Research shows that living-wage laws (laws that set the minimum wage for a city or county at a higher level than the federal minimum wage) harm unskilled workers. These laws either result in employers laying off workers to compensate for higher payroll expenses or in companies hiring only skilled workers in order to make hires more cost-effective. Furthermore, such legislation is unnecessary because most minimum wage workers are young people who are just entering the workforce and will soon move on to other jobs that pay better wages. Rather than casting employers as greedy, advocates for the poor would do better to encourage workers to gain skills and education that will make them more employable.

For nearly a decade, activists on the left have been conducting a highly effective nationwide campaign to mandate local minimum wages at levels that presumably eliminate poverty for full-time workers and their families. This "living wage," as it is known, is now the law in dozens of jurisdictions, and dozens

Carl F. Horowitz, "Keeping the Poor Poor: The Dark Side of the Living Wage," *Policy Analysis*, vol. 493, October 21, 2003, pp. 3–9. Copyright © 2003 by the Cato Institute. All rights reserved. Reproduced by permission.

more are actively considering similar measures. Typically, a living wage is set anywhere from 50 percent to 100 percent above the current federal minimum wage of $5.15 an hour and often higher if employees do not provide health benefits. Thus far, there has been only modest resistance, even from local governments for which the cost of doing business inevitably rises.

Most living wage ordinances apply to private-sector government contractors and, to a lesser extent, recipients of business aid or local government employees, or both. Supporters insist that the benefits are enormous and the costs minimal. But that view is an illusion, a product of the insular world of local government contracting. If the living wage were applied to all employees across the United States—the goal of advocates of a living wage—it would greatly magnify the well-documented pitfalls of the minimum wage.

Decades of research have shown that the minimum wage harms the least-skilled workers from poor families while heavily benefiting young workers from middle-income households. Several studies critical of the living wage come to similar conclusions. The main beneficiaries of the living wage are public-sector unionized employees because of the reduced incentives for local governments to contract out work. Instead of exploiting grievances of the marginally employed against "greedy" employers, advocates for the poor should focus their energies on building the skills of the poor.

The "Age of the Living Wage"

The "age of the living wage" has arrived with a vengeance. [Since the mid-1990s], a well-organized coalition of community groups, labor unions, political parties, think tanks, and churches has coaxed dozens of local governments across the United States into forcing designated employers to pay workers well above the current federal minimum wage of $5.15 an hour. Living wage jurisdictions include major cities such as New York, Los Angeles, Chicago, and Baltimore plus a large number of smaller cities and suburban counties. Local school boards and institutions of higher learning are participating as well. By the end of 2002 there were 103 living wage measures on the books, enacted mostly by municipal and county general governments, and another 74 campaigns actively under way.

Activists defend living wage laws as protecting vulnerable entry-level workers from poverty. They also argue that such laws improve employee morale and productivity, which in turn improves employers' profits. Local governments, to the extent they pay contractors living wages, deliver better services at lower cost. Residents are more satisfied with the quality of life, and the pathologies associated with poverty are reduced. Only exploitative employers and their political supporters lose. Common sense and human decency therefore require national as well as local action in the face of right-wing scare tactics. The federal minimum wage should be made a "living" wage.

> *Instead of exploiting grievances of the marginally employed against 'greedy' employers, advocates for the poor should focus their energies on building the skills of the poor.*

The reality is quite different. At best, living wage laws bring about modest benefits at a higher cost to businesses and taxpayers. There should be little surprise in that. As an elevated version of the minimum wage, the living wage magnifies the former's labor market distortions. If applied to all employers in the United States, the living wage would make it far more difficult for first-time job seekers, especially those coming off welfare, to find work. The economic case for the living wage is difficult to make. Indeed, some three-fourths of economists surveyed by the Washington-based Employment Policies Institute said that living wage laws would result in employers looking for more-skilled employees, thus crowding out the people with the least skills—the very people whom living wage laws are intended to benefit.

More than Minimum Wage

A living wage differs from a minimum wage in several ways. First, a living wage is a good deal higher than the current federal minimum wage of $5.15 an hour and usually even the (higher) state minimum levels. Dozens of ordinances mandate that affected employers offer health benefits or pay a higher wage in lieu of benefits. To take one example, Cincinnati passed a living wage ordinance in 2002 requiring affected businesses to pay a living wage of $8.70 with health benefits or

$10.20 without. New York City's living wage, passed in 1996, mandates that for-profit contractors involved in security, cleaning, food, and temporary services pay employees minimum rates set annually by the city comptroller that may reach levels far above the wage in Cincinnati.

Second, living wage laws apply, and campaigns to enact them take place, at the local rather than state or federal level. Cities, counties, school boards, and, lately, colleges and universities have enacted living wage policies. Efforts to secure equivalent laws at the state or federal level have not been successful thus far.

Third, living wage laws cover far fewer employers than minimum wage rules. Ordinances apply mainly to private-sector government contractors, business recipients of economic development assistance, and local government employees. Only the ordinance enacted by the city of Santa Monica, California, covers employers generally, and even in that instance it operates within a restricted geographic area. That is why living wage laws, as of 2002, directly affected only about 1 percent of workers in conmunities that have such laws. . . .

> *At best, living wage laws bring about modest benefits at a higher cost to businesses and taxpayers.*

The current living wage campaign has its origins in the efforts of a church-led group, Baltimoreans United in Leadership Development, in alliance with the American Federation of State, County, and Municipal Employees. In Los Angeles a rabbi, an Episcopal bishop, and a Methodist bishop cowrote in a *Los Angeles Times* guest editorial, "We have a right and responsibility to see that . . . employees are paid enough to support themselves and their families in basic dignity." In their book, *The Living Wage: Building a Fair Economy*, advocates Robert Pollin and Stephanie Luce quote Deuteronomy 24:14 as an epigraph: "Thou shalt not oppress a hired servant that is poor and needy.". . .

The living wage thus far has been localized and limited to selected employers, but supporters want to institute it nationally and apply it to as many employers as possible. Fully realized, today's living wage would become tomorrow's minimum wage. . . .

Displaced Workers

More than 80 studies have demonstrated a link between an increase in the minimum wage and subsequent job loss, especially among teenagers and unskilled adults, the workers with the least skills, experience, and education. The more employers have to pay such workers, the less likely they are to employ them. Those workers may turn out to be productive employees, but they present risks to the employer so, given the minimum price set by the state, the employer reduces risk by hiring only more-qualified workers. Hyundais are less reliable automobiles than Hondas or Toyotas. If the Hyundais could not compete on the basis of a lower price, none would be bought. . . .

> *The more employers have to pay such workers, the less likely they are to employ them.*

Adult welfare recipients in particular are susceptible to the crowding-out problem. Overwhelmingly, they are single mothers with children and far more often than other women had not completed high school at the time of the birth of their first child. Some two-fifths of all women on welfare have no work experience prior to going on welfare. At least a third are functionally illiterate.

Peter Brandon of the University of Wisconsin's Institute for Research on Poverty concluded several years ago that raising the minimum wage is not an effective way to remove families from the welfare rolls. The average length of time spent receiving welfare benefits was 13.5 months in states that did not raise their wage floor but 19.5 months, or nearly 45 percent longer, in states that did raise the minimum.

Poor Policy

Advocates of the living wage argue that it combats poverty, but the evidence does not support that claim.

First, the problem for low-income Americans is really insufficient hours rather than insufficient wages. A Bureau of Labor Statistics report revealed that in 2000 only 3.5 percent of all household heads who worked full-time 27 weeks or more over the course of the year fell below the poverty line. By contrast, this figure was 10.2 percent for household heads who worked less than 27 weeks. The BLS study also revealed that only a few more than 20 percent of all household heads with below-poverty-line incomes attributed their condition solely to low earnings. The remaining 80 percent cited unemployment, involuntary part-time employment, or one or both of those factors in combination with low earnings. In addition, the Census Bureau reported that the median income in 1999 for household heads working full-time year-round (50 weeks or more) was $55,619. By contrast, household heads working full-time 27 to 49 weeks had a median income of only $38,868, and for those who worked full-time 26 weeks or less the figure was $26,001. An Employment Policies Institute analysis of 1995 Census Current Population Survey data concluded that only 44 percent of minimum wage employees worked full time.

> *The problem for low-income Americans is really insufficient hours rather than insufficient wages.*

Second, most of the intended beneficiaries of a minimum wage hike do not come from poor households. EPI's analysis showed that at most 13.3 percent of minimum wage employees were the sole breadwinners of below-poverty-line family. And all such families (and many above them in income as well) are eligible for the Earned Income Tax Credit. The EITC, which began in the mid-1970s as a pilot program, now adds well over $30 billion a year to the take-home pay of low- and moderate-income families. The 1997 federal tax reform legislation also created a $500 per child tax credit, which Congress later raised to $600 and most recently to $1,000 in 2003.

Finally, a low-wage family's situation is not likely to be permanent. Family heads who earn the minimum wage are typically no older than 30 years of age. EPI research with Census data revealed that only 2.8 percent of employees older than 30 worked at or below the minimum wage. In fact, the average income of minimum wage employees of all ages increased 30 percent within one year of employment.

Only 3 percent of the nation's workers make the minimum wage or less, a proportion that drops to only 1.5 percent of full-time workers, according to Bureau of Labor Statistics data. Some 85 percent of employees whose wages would be increased by a minimum wage hike from $5.15 to $6.15 an hour live with their parents or another relative, live alone, or have a working spouse. About half of those persons—42 percent— were in the first category. Thus only 15 percent of minimum wage workers had to support a family, whether as a single parent or as a single earner in a couple with children. . . .

Gains and Losses

Michigan State University's David Neumark has done the most significant research to date on the impact of the living wage. He analyzed data on more than 20 large- and medium-sized cities across the nation in which living wage laws have been enacted. His econometric analyses controlled for as many variables as possible to determine whether factors other than living wage laws could have affected employment and wage levels among low-wage workers.

> *A low-wage family's situation is not likely to be permanent.*

He concluded that the living wage does raise the wages of low-wage workers. If a living wage is set at 50 percent above the minimum wage, the average wage for workers in the bottom tenth of the wage distribution increases by 3.5 percent. The living wage at that level would lower the local poverty rate by 1.8 percentage points. But that, he cautioned, was only part of the story. For living wage laws also reduce employment among affected workers. A living wage set at 50 percent above the minimum wage would reduce the employment rate for people in the bottom tenth of predicted wage distribution by 7 percent, or 2.8 percentage points. "These disemployment effects." he wrote, "counter the positive effect of living wage laws on the wages of low-wage workers, pointing to the tradeoff between wages and employment that economic theory would predict." The primary beneficiaries of living wage laws, he also concluded, are likely to be public employees' unions. By reducing the incentives for cities to contract out work, those ordinances increase the bargaining power of the unions, indirectly leading to higher wages. . . .

Seeking Skills

The word "skill" implies knowledge of how to do something competently. The more complicated the tasks, the more the person performing them can be said skilled. Yet in the context of labor policy, a skill, more broadly, is any attribute of an employee that can lend value to the employer's bottom line. It includes not only the ability to handle basic job procedures but also such character traits as punctuality, openness to learning, and an ability to cooperate with, and lend assistance to, coworkers.

If a worker possesses unusual skills, and demonstrates them at or even beyond expectations, an employer will make the extra effort to retain that worker—and perhaps even pay him more than the competition would. By contrast, if a worker's skills, or ability to apply them, are commonplace, the employer will be less likely to raise his wages. Character traits also affect a worker's value to an employer. Even the most technically adept workers may find themselves out of jobs if they display excessive absenteeism or are repeatedly uncooperative.

The low-wage labor force is, by definition, a labor force lacking some combination of education, training, job experience, and social skills. To raise wages *and* boost productivity, public policy ought to focus on encouraging low-wage workers to gain skills. Creating and raising a floor wage, divorced from such a consideration, makes the least-skilled workers more dispensable than ever. But that would seem at odds with the primary purpose of the living wage, which is to *protect* the most vulnerable individuals and families. . . .

> *Living wage laws also reduce employment among affected workers.*

Only 5 percent of U.S. households in the bottom fifth of the income distribution in 1975, revealed W. Michael Cox and Richard Alm in their book, *Myths of Rich & Poor*, were still there in 1991. Nearly 3 in 10 of those lowest-income households had moved up to the top fifth over that period. In the early 1990s the median duration of poverty was 4.2 months; only a third of the roughly 36 million Americans living in poverty had been below the poverty line for 24 or more months. Advocates of a living wage fail to grasp the reality that poverty is more often than not a transition phase for persons able and willing to work.

Overlooking Education

Advocates of a living wage likewise overlook the role of education in boosting earnings, and not just for the "richest" Americans. Full-time, year-round workers aged 25–64 earned the following annual amounts (in 1999 dollars) during the period 1997–99: Persons lacking a high school diploma earned on average only $23,400. Earnings for those with high school diplomas rose to $30,400. For those whose highest levels of educational attainment were some college but no degree, an associate's degree, and a bachelor's degree, respectively, the figures were $36,800, $38,200, and $52,200. Moreover, the long-term trend for well over two decades has indicated that educational level makes an increasing difference. The most educated persons, concluded the Hudson Institute's *Workforce 2020* report, experienced the greatest gains in annual real earnings during 1975–94, whereas the earnings of those who did not complete their high school education *declined* slightly over that period.

> *Advocates of a living wage likewise overlook the role of education in boosting earnings, and not just for the 'richest' Americans.*

Companies know the value of hiring educated workers. A University of Pennsylvania study showed that a 10 percent increase in the educational level of an employer's workforce increased productivity by 8.6 percent; a 10 percent rise in hours worked and investment in capital equipment hiked productivity, respectively, by only 5.6 percent and 3.4 percent. Data from the Bureau of Labor Statistics show that on average 28-year-old workers who tested in the top quartile of math skills on the National Assessment of Educational Progress earned 37 percent more than those in lower quartiles.

Even some economists in the egalitarian camp understand

that. Lester Thurow, an MIT economist on the board of the Economic Policy Institute, has written: "For individuals here are three words of advice: skills, skills, skills. The economic prospects of those without skills are bleak." A Clinton-era Commerce Department monograph also cited the need for skills, adding that globalization, the end of the Cold War, and the spread of emerging information technologies could further jeopardize the prospects of unskilled workers. Robert Shapiro, director of economic studies for the Progressive Policy Institute and a key adviser to Bill Clinton's 1992 presidential campaign, wrote: "[B]y *not* building new knowledge and skills, many working people see their economic capacities slowly depreciate over the course of every year, leaving them relatively less productive and efficient—and less well-paid."

The Wrong Focus

People who push for a living wage insist that the lowest-paid workers are victims of social injustice rectifiable through aggressive political action. They are wrong. The lowest-paid members of the workforce suffer from a lack of skills. In 1994 the Labor and Commerce Departments issued a joint report warning of a widening underclass of workers unable to compete in a complex marketplace. The report spoke of "a large, growing population for whom illegal activity is more attractive than legitimate work."

> *It is time for local elected officials to resist a living wage movement that is likely to harm America's poor in the name of protecting them.*

Organizations such as ACORN stand ready to exploit the discontent of the poor in recruiting them for political cadres. The larger the cadres, moreover, the easier it is for living wage activities to intimidate and shame political opponents as "enemies of the poor." And what local government official wants to be known as an enemy of the poor? Experience bears that out. When the Chicago City Council voted in 1908 to require for profit city contractors to pay workers in selected occupations a $7.60 an hour living wage, the measure passed 49 to 0. When the New York City Council in 1996 voted 42 to 5 to override Mayor Giuliani's earlier veto of a living wage bill, even opponents conceded that they faced an uphill climb at best. "This was a battle we could not have won in a million years," said one city official. "Council made it look like we were the rich Republicans from the mayor's office, and they were protecting the little guy.

The living wage campaign is a triumph of confrontation politics and class resentment. By framing the issue as the poor vs. employers, proponents have convinced many local public officials that their campaign is an overdue and unstoppable juggernaut for social justice. It is time for local elected officials to resist a living wage movement that is likely to harm America's poor in the name of protecting them.

7

Improving the Poor's Financial Knowledge Will Help Alleviate Poverty in the United States

Annamaria Lusardi

Annamaria Lusardi is associate professor of economics at Dartmouth College.

Many low-income families do not have savings and are therefore less likely to be able to absorb financial shocks and plan for retirement. Without bank accounts, they are also unable to build the credit records that would help them purchase a house or get a loan to start a business. Government agencies should promote initiatives, such as teaching students about the benefits of saving, to improve financial literacy among the poor.

It is a long-standing puzzle why so many low-income families do not save and hold little or no assets. Often these families, which are disproportionately single-parent black or Hispanic and headed by those with little education, do not hold wealth at any stage of their life. Thus, not only have poor families little to rely on for their retirement, but they also have no buffer to shield against shocks when young or middle aged. One of the important determinants of saving behavior is financial lit-

Annamaria Lusardi, "Increasing Saving Among the Poor: The Role of Financial Literacy," *Poverty Research News,* vol. 6, January/February 2002. Copyright © 2002 by the Joint Center for Poverty Research. Reproduced by permission.

eracy, and public policies that aim to increase financial security among the poor should find ways to remove this major obstacle to saving.

Studies have shown that many low-income families not only have no stocks, Individual Retirement Accounts (IRAs), or bonds, but they also hold no basic assets, such as checking or saving accounts. About 10 million Americans have no bank accounts. They pay hefty fees to cash checks or pay bills, and more important, they are not building the credit records needed, for example, to buy a house or to secure a loan to start a business.

Financial Literacy

One of the reasons why poor people do not save is that they lack experience and expertise in dealing with financial matters. Financial illiteracy is particularly acute among the poor, and women, in particular, report having little financial knowledge. A growing number of employers have launched initiatives to promote financial literacy, from distributing brochures to information sessions and retirement seminars. The Department of Labor has launched a national pension education program aimed at "drawing the attention of American workers to the importance of taking personal responsibility for their retirement security."

Although these initiatives are important and document how widespread the problem of financial illiteracy is, they are unlikely to affect the poor. Minority groups, single mothers, and individuals with little education are unlikely to work at firms that offer such initiatives.

One of the important determinants of saving behavior is financial literacy.

The poor are not only excluded from employer-sponsored initiatives, but they are also unlikely to benefit from the experience of others around them. Several recent studies show that family background plays an important role in the amount and type of assets households own. Individuals, and women in particular, learn about financial matters from parents and siblings.

Reaching Low-Income Families

Reaching out to low-income families may be particularly difficult and, as the experience of employers shows, mailing a book-
let of information is likely ineffective. Government institutions
that provide support to the poor, however, can promote initiatives to improve financial literacy, as well as provide simple and
basic financial advice on-site. Government agencies in charge of
unemployment benefits or welfare programs, charities aimed at
supporting the poor, and social workers could promote initiatives on financial education aimed explicitly to the poor.

> *One of the reasons why poor people do not
> save is that they lack experience and expertise in
> dealing with financial matters.*

These initiative should aim to:
- Demonstrate the advantages of saving;
- Explain the costs incurred in the lack of saving and the
  money management practices chosen by poor families,
  such as check cashing shops, pawn shops, payday loans,
  and purchases on installments;
- Suggest how to implement saving decisions and, thus,
  how to take steps to start saving and use banks and traditional financial markets.

Knowledge Is Power

Each of these pieces of a financial education program is important. The benefits of saving may not be apparent to families
that have never saved. Similarly, the costs incurred with different methods of saving and borrowing are often unknown to
those who have never consulted a bank or invested in financial
assets. Finally, providing clear suggestions on how to implement saving decisions as well as money management is very
important. There is some anecdotal evidence that poor families
fear or distrust banks, and they are unaware of the effective interest rate charged by payday loans. In addition, families may
need commitment devices other than cash savings (such as
signing up for direct deposit or automatic transfers, etc.) because visible cash savings may tempt families to spend it.

Another useful initiative is to institute educational policies in school about saving. Again, teaching about the benefits of saving and the actions needed to save may be very important for children in families that have never saved. These children can, in turn, teach their parents, providing another way to reach families.

There is growing evidence that financial education has an effect on saving. For example, retirement seminars are found to affect both the level of saving and the way households allocate their portfolios. Similarly, children exposed to financial education in school are found to have higher saving in their adulthood. Thus, to be effective, public policies should aim to promote not only tax incentives for saving, but also the understanding of the benefits of saving. Some of the education policies implemented to date have aimed at the population at large; however, to be even more effective, they should be targeted to the segment of the population where saving is scarce.

8

Redefining Poverty Will Help America's Poor

Hilary Silver and S.M. Miller

Hilary Silver is a professor of sociology and urban studies at Brown University in Providence, Rhode Island. S.M. Miller is a research professor of sociology at Boston College and coauthor of Respect and Rights: Race, Class and Gender Today.

The United States bases its poverty line on a rule developed in 1964 that measures income and only identifies people living in the most difficult material circumstances as poor. In contrast the countries of the European Union (EU) measure poverty by determining how the poor are faring compared to the rest of society while also recognizing that beyond having money, the poor also need access to housing, health care, education, and jobs to escape poverty. America should follow the EU's lead and redefine poverty in terms of social exclusion by looking at issues such as access to insurance, schools, child care, and affordable housing.

The United States is falling further behind the European Union in its conceptualization and measurement of poverty and its understanding of those living at the margins of society. The U.S. still imagines poverty strictly as a deficiency of income for basic necessities. In contrast, the European Union has continually revised its thinking about social deprivation, adopting a view of poverty relative to rising average living standards and, more recently, building a framework for thinking about nonmonetary aspects of deprivation. Europeans are now committed

Hilary Silver and S.M. Miller, "Social Exclusion: The European Approach to Social Disadvantage," *Poverty and Race*, September/October 2002, pp. 3–8. Copyright © 2002 by the Poverty & Race Research Action Council. Reproduced by permission.

to include the "excluded," the outsiders, the people left out of mainstream society and left behind in a globalizing economy. The U.S. can learn much from the European fight against social exclusion. A new agenda for political action could emerge.

Ironically, an Englishman, B. Seebohm Rowntree, at the end of the 19th Century, pioneered the American method of counting the poor by estimating an absolute monetary threshold based upon bare subsistence requirements. Our poverty line reflects a convenient rule of thumb that a government economist, Mollie Orshansky, devised in 1964. It has since become a policy and social science fixture. Based on the value of an "economy food plan" times three (since at this time the average family of three spent a third of its after-tax income on food), this narrow approach persists, even though today food, including restaurant meals, accounts for only 13.5% of annual budgets for that family size and 14.9% of expenditures by the poorest 20% of families. The poverty threshold, adjusted only for inflation, identifies people living in the direst material circumstances, not those living below what John Kenneth Galbraith termed "the grades and standards" of society. Although in 1995 the National Academy of Sciences recommended limited changes to the poverty line in order to reflect real consumption relative to all money and non-monetary resources, minus work-related expenses, there has as yet been no official redefinition. . . .

> // The U.S. still imagines poverty strictly as a deficiency of income for basic necessities. //

In contrast, the European Union adopted as the official poverty line a *relative* poverty indicator: one-half or less of the national median disposable household income. It rises when Europeans grow richer. EU statistical reports provide data on 50% and 60% of median income, offering evidence of near poverty as well. Concern about rising income inequality, a problem much worse in the U.S. than in Europe, has also encouraged the development of income distribution measures. The European Household Panel Survey the 1980s, as the problem groups "excluded" from economic growth multiplied, "exclusion" discourse helped cement a national movoverty, tracking those who enter, leave and stay mired in destitution.

Indicators of Social Exclusion

At the March 2001 Stockholm Summit, the European Commission's Synthesis Report on Social Inclusion proposed seven indicators of "social exclusion," three of which captured forms of "financial poverty": (1) the share of the population below 60% of national median income (adjusted for household size) before and after social transfers; (2) the ratio of the share of the top 20% to the share of the bottom 20% of the income distribution; and (3) persistent poverty, or the share of the population below the 60% poverty line for the current year and at least two of the preceding three years.

> *The most significant European innovation is the development of non-monetary indicators of 'social exclusion,' transcending economists' focus on money.*

The most significant European innovation is the development of non-monetary indicators of "social exclusion," transcending economists' focus on money. Mention of "social exclusion" in European public and social science discourse has increased much faster than references to "poverty" or "the underclass." Cognizant that deprivation is a multi-dimensional condition, Eurostat (the EU Statistical Office), national statistical agencies and European social scientists have developed social and political benchmarks to track progress against exclusion.

Europeans conceive of social exclusion as distinct from income poverty. Poverty is a distributional outcome, whereas exclusion is a relational process of declining participation, solidarity and access. For some, exclusion is a broader term encompassing poverty; for others, it is a cause or a consequence of poverty. The two may even be unrelated. . . .

The European Experience

Most policies promoting social inclusion or cohesion . . . emphasize: (1) multi-pronged interventions crossing traditional bureaucratic domains and tailored to the multi-dimensional problems of excluded individuals and groups; (2) a long-term process of insertion and integration moving through transitional stages; and (3) participation of the excluded in their own inclusion into economic and social life. The latter is especially important since targeted and means-tested programs may stigmatize their intended beneficiaries. Often, local nonprofit initiatives of disadvantaged residents become public-private partnerships supported with subsidies from municipal or national governments and the European Union Structural Funds.

> *Europeans conceive of social exclusion as distinct from income poverty.*

The number of unemployed workers in the EU soared from 14 million in 1992 to 16.5 million in 1998, half of whom were out of work for over a year. These dismal facts and the urging of France and other countries forced the EU to recognize that its economic market integration had a "social dimension" too. Drawing upon lessons from building monetary union and committed to "basic principles of solidarity which should remain the trademark of Europe," the "Luxembourg Process" coordinated a European Employment Strategy of 19 guidelines into four pillars: (1) improving employability; (2) developing entrepreneurship; (3) encouraging business and worker adaptability; and (4) equal employment opportunity. The Employment Strategy was "soft law," integrating EU, national and local level efforts through peer pressure and without recourse to regulations with formal sanctions. Multi-level iterative monitoring promotes learning from national best practices and modification of goals and procedures. Explicit long-term employment targets were later adopted. In December 2000, the EU applied this "open coordination method" to social policy, separating the fight against poverty and exclusion from employment strategy more generally. Every two years, nation-states produce "National Action Plans" on social inclusion, laying out their progress towards agreed-upon goals on a variety of social indicators.

Since 2000, the European Council has pursued a comprehensive strategy to become the "most competitive and dynamic knowledge-based economy," combining "sustainable economic growth with more and better jobs and greater social cohesion." To this end, European social policy explicitly aims to eradicate poverty, fight social exclusion and enhance social cohesion. In October 2001, the European Commission and the Council adopted the Joint Inclusion Report, based upon the first 2001 National Action Plans of Social Inclusion. The document, which strongly resembles the 1998 French law against social exclusion, specified four objectives:

- *Facilitating participation in employment and access to resources and rights, goods and services for all citizens* (e.g., social protection, housing, health care, education, justice, culture);
- *Preventing the risks of exclusion* by preserving family solidarity, preventing over indebtedness and homelessness, and promoting equal access to new technologies;
- *Helping the most vulnerable* (e.g., the persistently poor, children, residents of areas marked by exclusion);
- *Mobilizing all relevant bodies* by promoting participation and self-expression of the excluded and partnerships and mainstreaming their concerns. . . .

Implications for the United States

American politicians have always resisted a relative definition of poverty. Poverty line thinking has so dominated American social policy that "welfare" has narrowed its meaning to means-tested income transfers to lone parents. Now that welfare "reform" has mobilized multiple social supports to enable these parents to enter the paid labor force, the rhetoric of "inclusion"—the demand for access to jobs, respect and a place at the table—may not sound as foreign as it once did.

> *American politicians have always resisted a relative definition of poverty.*

How many working Americans are "excluded" from health, unemployment or disability insurance? How many are excluded from good jobs because of inadequate family support or child care or inferior public schools? How many are shut out of the housing market by unaffordable rents? Isn't segregation about exclusion from white and "better" neighborhoods, schools, suburbs? Has the Americans with Disabilities Act really eliminated physical exclusion from all public facilities? Are not formally equal citizens denied a say, while politicians listen mainly to campaign contributors and school officials listen only to English?

If social exclusion and inclusion became important ideas in U.S. thinking, alongside concerns with absolute poverty, the political landscape might begin to change. Currently, groups concerned about neighborhoods (crime, services, education), the labor market (low wages, insecure employment, long-term unemployment, contingent work, unemployment insurance), social programs and services (Medicaid, Temporary Assistance to Needy Families, food stamps, child care), school performance, immigration and many other issues are fragmented and even competitive. A social exclusion/inclusion approach could serve as the rhetorical umbrella that brings the groups together politically and strategically.

The role of symbolic discourse in building political alliances should not be underestimated. Talking about "exclusion" connects people at all levels of the society through a common emotional experience found in social relations everywhere. No one can get through life without some rejection, humiliation or unfair treatment. We have all been subjected to sanctions like gossip, or felt unwanted, left out, stigmatized or "dissed." The goal of inclusion appeals to our democratic impulses and common humanity, promoting solidarity with the excluded.

Battling Bureaucracy

Just as "social exclusion" highlights the complex multi-dimensionality and cumulative character of social disadvantage, so must inclusionary policies transcend traditional bureaucratic domains. Discrete programs and single-focus policies that now administer to people in need are, to put it euphemistically, disjointed. Service providers have little contact with one another. Families with multiple problems must make the rounds among many bureaucracies operating in different ways, each with scant understanding of families' overall situation. Americans need more comprehensive, "transversal" or what the British call "joined-up policies for joined-up problems" across social policy domains. Britain's Social Exclusion Unit and France's "inter-ministerial" commissions connect national policy areas across agencies. Regional and local public-private partnerships collectively administer social assistance and service programs. One-stop service centers and casework that tailors packages of support and assistance to individual needs are back in vogue. In the U.S., more progressive states now pursue similar strategies in their welfare-to-work policies, but integrating [the Temporary Assistance to Needy Families government welfare program] (TANF) with the Workforce Improvement Act and human services should be national policy.

> *The great divides of American society are not only economic but are also based on racial-ethnic, gender, cultural, educational and political status lines.*

The great divides of American society are not only economic but are also based on racial-ethnic, gender, cultural, educational and political status lines. Discrimination and disrespect have material consequences, denying access to information, contacts and resources, consigning minorities to low-quality schools, dangerous neighborhoods, poorly paid jobs and even joblessness. Americanizing the social exclusion perspective could put new wind in the sails of affirmative action. Calling for full inclusion would show that poverty, racism and other forms of domination are integral to the functioning of American society, rather than accidental or unintended consequences easily addressed with an ameliorative program or financial adjustment here or there.

To be sure, there is a danger of ghettoization and stigmatization whenever we introduce new labels for social problems. Calling attention to spectacular forms of cumulative disadvantage may distract attention from widespread problems like rising inequality and family dissolution and undermine broader social programs. Indeed, some on the European Left worry that the "social exclusion" framework is replacing a "social class" perspective. Any discourse can serve a variety of political purposes, but insuring widespread participation may overcome these downsides. Although people argue about the precise nature and measures of exclusion and cohesion, these ideas do provide a framework for discussing the new, complex forms of disadvantage. Easily understood indicators could be found for these notions. Benchmarking our progress as a society could go beyond the simple, intuitive and familiar poverty line to track multiple forms of disadvantage. A new politics might emerge.

9

Globalization Has Helped Reduce Poverty Worldwide

International Chamber of Commerce

Founded in 1919, the International Chamber of Commerce is an international business organization that promotes market economies and an open international trade and investment system.

Many critics claim that globalization increases the gap between rich and poor and makes living conditions worse for the poor, but research shows that poverty rates and income inequality have declined as globalization has increased. Indeed, economic inequality has decreased in most globalizing developing countries. Globalization has also helped improve the living standards of many of the world's poorest people, decreased the number of undernourished people, and boosted life expectancy throughout the world. The exception to many of these statistics is Africa, where poverty is getting worse, although some African economies are showing signs of progress. Globalization presents an opportunity for all the world's people to prosper.

In the debate over globalization, it is often claimed that the gap between rich and poor has kept widening over recent decades and that the living conditions of the poor have deteriorated as a result of globalization. But new research now disproves such claims, shedding a much more favourable light on the contribution of global economic integration to incomes and income distribution. This new research shows that, contrary to popular belief, it is precisely during the recent period of increased globalization of the world economy that poverty rates and global income inequality have most diminished. . . .

In a paper entitled *Global Income Inequality: Beliefs, Facts and Unresolved Issues*, Arne Melchior, from the Norwegian Institute of International Affairs, warns against reaching hasty conclusions about inequality between countries. Many poor countries, especially in Africa, have experienced falling income during recent years. But, as Melchior says, "it is also true that a significant number of poor or formerly poor countries, including the world's two most populous countries, China and India, as well as other large developing countries, particularly but not only in Asia, have grown faster than the richest group of nations". China and India account for 38% of the world's population. Once weighted by population, the measure of income inequality shows that many developing countries are actually converging toward the richest countries' living standards.

> **It is precisely during the recent period of increased globalization of the world economy that poverty rates and global income inequality have most diminished.**

Inequalities have increased within several countries with high levels of growth over recent years. Yet, this should not overshadow the significant progress made in terms of raising incomes and living standards for the large majority of the population of these countries. A World Bank publication, *Globalization, Growth, and Poverty: Building an Inclusive World Economy* notes that, while inequality in most of the globalizing developing countries—such as Malaysia or the Philippines—has declined since 1980, rapid economic growth in China has widened the gap between rural and urban areas. But as the report points out, "if this increase in inequality in China has been the price of growth, it has paid off in terms of massive reduction in poverty."

The very fact that countries with comparable levels of growth have experienced different trends in income distribution also shows that there is no direct relation between globalization and inequality within countries. Income distribution in a given country primarily depends on domestic factors such as economic policy choices and redistribution mechanisms.

Moving Towards Equal Incomes

While it is true that inequality has increased in some countries and fallen in others, there is a clear trend towards convergence in world income distribution between individuals, i.e., regardless of their country. In *The World Distribution of Income (estimated from individual country distributions)*, [Xavier] Sala-i-Martin uses nine different indexes to measure global income inequality (or world inter-personal inequality). All of them show that there has been a substantial narrowing of the gap between rich and poor during the last two decades.

A report published by the Australian Department of Foreign Affairs and Trade, *Globalization and Poverty: Turning the Corner*, reaches similar conclusions by comparing the frequency distribution of global income (Lorenz curve) in 1965 and 1997. The authors found greater income equality in 1997 than in the mid-1960s. . . .

Poverty Has Declined

Contrary to what is often repeated, globalization has contributed to unprecedented advances in increasing the living conditions of many of the world's poorest people. New research by Xavier Sala-i-Martin shows that absolute poverty and poverty rates have both substantially declined over the last 30 years. On a global scale, the proportion of people living on less than a dollar a day has fallen from 20% to 5% over the last 25 years. The *two*-dollar-a-day poverty rate dropped from 44% to 18% of world population. In Asia, the proportion of people living on less than two dollars a day has dropped from 60% in 1970 to 17% in 2000, lifting more than 650 million people out of deep poverty.

Countries like Indonesia, Bangladesh, Uganda and Vietnam have all succeeded in sharply reducing poverty over the last decade. Dramatic decreases in poverty rates took place in Indonesia, with just 3% of the population living on less than two dollars a day in 1998 compared with 69% in 1970. This was also the case in Bangladesh, where the proportion of people living on less than two dollars a day has dropped by a quarter since

1970. In Vietnam, 98% of the poorest 5% of households in 1992 were better off six years later, according to a paper entitled *Spreading the Wealth* by David Dollar and Aart Kraay. Poverty in Uganda fell by 40% during the 1990s. In India, in spite of controversy over different poverty measurement methods, poverty rates have also been shown to be declining.

> **❝** *There has been a substantial narrowing of the gap between rich and poor during the last two decades.* **❞**

When measuring poverty, it also important to take into account living standards and not just incomes. Here again, evidence tells us that, overall, quality of life has improved in the developing world. According to the Australian Department of Foreign Affairs and Trade, the number of undernourished people in the world has been reduced from 920 million in 1970 to 810 million today. The World Bank study says school enrollments in Uganda have doubled during the 1990s. In a study for the Brookings Institution Global Inequality Group, Gary Burtless shows that life expectancy has been rising almost everywhere in the world and that as a result "world inequality in the distribution of expected life spans has declined."

The Case of Africa

The purpose here is not to give a rosier picture than the real situation. Global income inequality and poverty rates have declined, but many countries have also suffered from increased marginalization and have been unable to reduce poverty and inequality over the last two decades. More than 40% of Africans live on less than a dollar a day, a rate that has been steadily increasing in the continent as a whole since the 1970s. Conflict and inappropriate policy choices persist in holding many African countries back from economic progress.

Nevertheless, several African economies show hopeful signs of progress. According to the latest [United Nations] report on Africa, *Economic Report on Africa 2002: Tracking Performance and Progress*, the majority of African countries achieved economic growth of more than 3% in 2001—although from a very low base—hence outperforming other developing regions. Since 1970, the proportion of people living on less than a dollar a day decreased in 13 African countries. Global integration is crucial for the recovery of African countries. Globalization must therefore be seen not as a threat to welfare but rather as an opportunity to achieve higher economic growth and rising incomes.

Business Is an Opportunity

The rapid economic progress of countries, and particularly developing countries, that have integrated into the global economy has shown the positive contribution that globalization can make by raising incomes and living standards throughout the world. Wealth creation through entrepreneurship, opening of export markets, flows of foreign direct investment and technology, and the resulting spiral of prosperity and job creation are the benefits that global economic integration can bring to developing nations.

The results so far are encouraging: poverty rates have decreased and global income inequality has diminished in recent decades. The challenge is now to enable the poorest countries to benefit from the opportunities of the global economy. . . . World business has a leading role to play in showing how globalization can be an opportunity for all and ensuring that necessary public actions are undertaken to create the conditions for growth and prosperity in these countries.

10

Globalization Has Not Yet Helped Reduce Poverty Worldwide

Joseph E. Stiglitz

Joseph E. Stiglitz is a Nobel Prize winner in economic science, former chairman of the Council of Economic Advisers in the Clinton administration, and former chief economist for the World Bank.

Globalization has helped to bring health, democracy, and social justice to many countries. However, not all of the world's poor have benefited. In order for globalization to be more beneficial for all, developed countries and international financial institutions must allow poor nations to set policies that are best for them. Moreover, developing nations must take responsibility for making sure that globalization benefits all their citizens, not just privileged groups. If steered in the right way, globalization could prove a potent remedy for poverty.

G lobalization today is not working for many of the world's poor. It is not working for much of the environment. It is not working for the stability of the global economy. The transition from communism to a market economy has been so badly managed that, with the exception of China, Vietnam, and a few Eastern European countries, poverty has soared as incomes have plummeted.

To some, there is an easy answer: Abandon globalization. That is neither feasible nor desirable. . . . Globalization has also brought huge benefits—East Asia's success was based on globalization, especially on the opportunities for trade, and increased access to markets and technology. Globalization has brought better health, as well as an active global civil society fighting for more democracy and greater social justice. The problem is not with globalization, but with how it has been managed. Part of the problem lies with the international economic institutions, with the IMF [International Monetary Fund], World Bank, and WTO [World Trade Organization], which help set the rules of the game. They have done so in ways that, all too often, have served the interests of the more advanced industrialized countries—and particular interests within those countries—rather than those of the developing world. But it is not just that they have served those interests; too often, they have approached globalization from particular narrow mind-sets, shaped by a particular vision of the economy and society.

Reform Is Needed

The demand for reform is palpable—from congressionally appointed commissions and foundation-supported groups of eminent economists writing reports on changes in the global financial architecture to the protests that mark almost every international meeting. In response, there has already been some change. The new round of trade negotiations that was agreed to in November 2001 at Doha, Qatar, has been characterized as the "development round," intended not just to open up markets further but to rectify some of the imbalances of the past, and the debate at Doha was far more open than in the past. The IMF and the World Bank have changed their rhetoric—there is much more talk about poverty, and at least at the World Bank, there is a sincere attempt to live up to its commitment to "put the country in the driver's seat" in its programs in many countries. But many of the critics of the international institutions are skeptical. They see the changes as simply the institutions facing the political reality that they *must* change their rhetoric if they are to survive. These critics doubt that there is real commitment. They were not reassured when, in 2000, the IMF appointed to its number two position someone who had been chief economist at the World Bank during the period when it took on market fundamentalist ideology. Some critics are so doubtful about these reforms that they continue to call for more drastic actions such as the abolition of the IMF, but I believe this is pointless. Were the Fund to be abolished, it would most likely be re-created in some other form. In times of international crises, government leaders like to feel there is someone in charge, that an international agency is doing something. Today, the IMF fills that role.

> *The problem is not with globalization, but with how it has been managed.*

I believe that globalization can be reshaped to realize its potential for good and I believe that the international economic institutions can be reshaped in ways that will help ensure that this is accomplished. But to understand how these institutions should be reshaped, we need to understand better why they have failed, and failed so miserably. . . .

Globalization with a Human Face

It is not just a question of changing institutional structures. The mind-set around globalization itself must change. Finance and trade ministers view globalization as largely an economic phenomenon; but to many in the developing world, it is far more than that.

One of the reasons globalization is being attacked is that it seems to undermine traditional values. The conflicts are real, and to some extent unavoidable. Economic growth—including that induced by globalization—will result in urbanization, undermining traditional rural societies. Unfortunately, so far, those responsible for managing globalization, while praising these positive benefits, all too often have shown an insufficient appreciation of this adverse side, the threat to cultural identity and values. This is surprising, given the awareness of the issues within the developed countries themselves: Europe defends its agricultural policies not just in terms of those special interests, but to preserve rural traditions. People in small towns everywhere complain that large national retailers and shopping malls have killed their small businesses and their communities.

The pace of global integration matters: a more gradual process means that traditional institutions and norms, rather than being overwhelmed, can adapt and respond to the new challenges.

Of equal concern is what globalization does to democracy. Globalization, as it has been advocated, often seems to replace the old dictatorships of national elites with new dictatorships of international finance. Countries are effectively told that if they don't follow certain conditions, the capital markets or the IMF will refuse to lend them money. They are basically forced to give up part of their sovereignty, to let capricious capital markets, including the speculators whose only concerns are short-term rather than the long-term growth of the country and the improvement of living standards, "discipline" them, telling them what they should and should not do.

Different Ways to Globalize

But countries do have choices, and among those choices is the extent to which they wish to subject themselves to international capital markets. Those, such as in East Asia, that have avoided the strictures of the IMF have grown faster, with greater equality and poverty reduction, than those who have obeyed its commandments. Because alternative policies affect different groups differently it is the role of the political process—not international bureaucrats—to sort out the choices. Even if growth *were* adversely affected, it is a cost many developing countries may be willing to pay to achieve a more democratic and equitable society, just as many societies today are saying it is worth sacrificing some growth for a better environment. So long as globalization is presented in the way that it has been, it represents a disenfranchisement. No wonder then that it will be resisted, especially by those who are being disenfranchised.

The Good and Bad of Globalization

Today, globalization is being challenged around the world. There is discontent with globalization, and rightfully so. Globalization can be a force for good: the globalization of ideas about democracy and of civil society have changed the way people think, while global political movements have led to debt relief and the treaty on land mines. Globalization has helped hundreds of millions of people attain higher standards of living, beyond what they, or most economists, thought imaginable but a short while ago. The globalization of the economy has benefited countries that took advantage of it by seeking new markets for their exports and by welcoming foreign investment. Even so, the countries that have benefited the most have been those that took charge of their own destiny and recognized the role government can play in development rather than relying on the notion of a self-regulated market that would fix its own problems.

But for millions of people globalization has not worked. Many have actually been made worse off, as they have seen their jobs destroyed and their lives become more insecure. They have felt increasingly powerless against forces beyond their control. They have seen their democracies undermined, their cultures eroded.

If globalization continues to be conducted in the way that it has been in the past, if we continue to fail to learn from our mistakes, globalization will not only not succeed in promoting development but will continue to create poverty and instability. Without reform, the backlash that has already started will mount and discontent with globalization will grow.

> **❝ I believe that globalization can be reshaped to realize its potential for good. ❞**

This will be a tragedy for all of us, and especially for the billions who might otherwise have benefited. While those in the developing world stand to lose the most economically, there will be broader political ramifications that will affect the developed world too. . . .

There is hope that a more humane process of globalization can be a powerful force for the good, with the vast majority of those living in the developing countries benefiting from it and welcoming it. If this is done, the discontent with globalization would have served us all well. . . .

Markets and Regulation

Thankfully, there is a growing recognition of these problems and increasing political will to do something. Almost everyone involved in development, even those in the Washington establishment, now agrees that rapid capital market liberalization without accompanying regulation can be dangerous. They agree too that the excessive tightness in fiscal policy in the

Asian crisis of 1997 was a mistake. As Bolivia moved into a recession in 2001, caused in part by the global economic slowdown, there were some intimations that that country would not be forced to follow the traditional path of austerity and have to cut governmental spending. Instead, as of January 2002, it looks like Bolivia will be allowed to stimulate its economy, helping it to overcome the recession, using revenues that it is about to receive from its newly discovered natural gas reserves to tide it over until the economy starts to grow again. In the aftermath of the Argentina debacle,[1] the IMF has recognized the failings of the big-bailout strategy and is beginning to discuss the use of standstills and restructuring through bankruptcy, the kinds of alternatives that I and others have been advocating for years. Debt forgiveness brought about by the work of the Jubilee movement and the concessions made to initiate a new development round of trade negotiations at Doha represent two more victories.

> *The mind-set around globalization itself must change.*

Despite these gains, there is still more to be done to bridge the gap between rhetoric and reality. At Doha, the developing countries only agreed to begin discussing a fairer trade agenda; the imbalances of the past have yet to be redressed. Bankruptcy and standstills are now on the agenda; but there is no assurance that there will be an appropriate balance of creditor and debtor interests. There is a lot more participation by those in developing countries in discussions concerning economic strategy, but there is little evidence yet of changes in policies that reflect greater participation. There need to be changes in institutions and in mind-sets. The free market ideology should be replaced with analyses based on economic science, with a more balanced view of the role of government drawn from an understanding of both market and government failures. There should be more sensitivity about the role of outside advisers, so they support democratic decision making by clarifying the

---

1. Argentina suffered a severe economic crisis in 2001 and 2002, with high rates of unemployment, a lengthy recession, and a default on foreign debts.

consequences of different policies, including impacts on different groups, especially the poor, rather than undermining it by pushing particular policies on reluctant countries.

A *Multipronged* Approach

It is clear that there must be a *multipronged* strategy of reform. One should be concerned with reform of the international economic arrangements. But such reforms will be a long time coming. Thus, the second prong should be directed at encouraging reforms that each country can take upon itself. The developed countries have a special responsibility, for instance, to eliminate their trade barriers, to practice what they preach. But while the developed countries' responsibility may be great, their incentives are weak: after all, off-shore banking centers and hedge funds serve interests in the developed countries, and the developed countries can withstand well the instability that a failure to reform might bring to the developing world. Indeed, the United States arguably benefited in several ways from the East Asia crisis.

Hence, the developing countries must assume responsibility for their well-being themselves. They can manage their budgets so that they live within their means, meager though that might be, and eliminate the protectionist barriers which, while they may generate large profits for a few, force consumers to pay higher prices. They can put in place strong regulations to protect themselves from speculators from the outside or corporate misbehavior from the inside. Most important, developing countries need effective governments, with strong and independent judiciaries, democratic accountability, openness and transparency and freedom from the corruption that has stifled the effectiveness of the public sector and the growth of the private.

> *Globalization has helped hundreds of millions of people attain higher standards of living.*

What they should ask of the international community is only this: the acceptance of their need, and right, to make their own choices, in ways which reflect their own political judgments about who, for instance, should bear what risks. They should be encouraged to adopt bankruptcy laws and regulatory structures adapted to their own situation, not to accept templates designed by and for the more developed countries.

The Reason for Development

What is needed are policies for sustainable, equitable, and democratic growth. This is the reason for development. Development is not about helping a few people get rich or creating a handful of pointless protected industries that only benefit the country's elite; it is not about bringing in Prada and Benetton, Ralph Lauren or Louis Vuitton, for the urban rich and leaving the rural poor in their misery. Being able to buy Gucci handbags in Moscow department stores did not mean that country had become a market economy. Development is about transforming societies, improving the lives of the poor, enabling everyone to have a chance at success and access to health care and education.

This sort of development won't happen if only a few people dictate the policies a country must follow. Making sure that democratic decisions are made means ensuring that a broad range of economists, officials, and experts from developing countries are actively involved in the debate. It also means that there must be broad participation that goes well beyond the experts and politicians. Developing countries must take charge of their own futures. But we in the West cannot escape our responsibilities.

It's not easy to change how things are done. Bureaucracies, like people, fall into bad habits, and adapting to change can be painful. But the international institutions must undertake the perhaps painful changes that will enable them to play the role they *should* be playing to make globalization work, and work not just for the well off and the industrial countries, but for the poor and the developing nations.

The developed world needs to do its part to reform the international institutions that govern globalization. We set up these institutions and we need to work to fix them. If we are to address the legitimate concerns of those who have expressed a discontent with globalization, if we are to make globalization work for the billions of people for whom it has not, if we are to make globalization with a human face succeed, then our voices must be raised. We cannot, we should not, stand idly by.

11

U.S. Foreign Aid Helps the World's Poor

David Beckmann

David Beckmann is a former World Bank economist, Lutheran clergyman, and the president of Bread for the World, a Christian organization that addresses hunger and poverty.

U.S. foreign aid to developing countries is very effective in combating poverty and raising the living standards of people in poor countries. However, critics continue to disseminate a number of myths about foreign aid. For example, some claim that foreign aid does not help the poor. This is untrue because while a great deal of U.S. foreign aid does not actually go to poor people, the aid that is focused on reducing poverty produces results nonetheless. Another myth is that aid gets lost to corrupt bureaucracies in developing countries. However, many U.S. agencies have become tougher on corruption. U.S. development assistance must be increased if global poverty and hunger are to be reduced further.

Fanny Makina, a farmer in Malawi, is tilling her plot of land with a hoe and spade. Next she will plant crops of corn, peanuts, squash, beans and cassava, and mark each row carefully with a stick. In most years, Makina harvests enough food for her family and has food left over to sell. Even in years of limited rainfall, she has income to buy fertilizer and other supplies.

"My children don't lack for clothes or shoes. I am able to pay their tuition for school," she says proudly. By Malawian standards, Makina is tremendously successful.

David Beckmann, "Not a Band-Aid," *The Christian Century*, vol. 118, August 1, 2001, p. 26. Copyright © 2001 by The Christian Century Foundation. Reproduced by permission.

Makina's success is due in part to U.S. foreign aid. She is a member of the National Smallholder Farmers Association of Malawi (NASFAM), an organization supported in part by the U.S. Agency for International Development (USAID). NASFAM farmers join together to learn about new agricultural methods and to negotiate better prices with truckers and with the merchants who buy their crops. Compared with other farmers, NASFAM members have higher incomes and are less likely to go without food in the annual "hungry time" before harvest.

For Makina and millions of others, aid-supported programs like NASFAM have made the difference. "People think Africa is a lost cause because we are so far away," says Makina. "But if they came and saw what we have achieved with the aid we are receiving, they would think otherwise."

> At the UN conferences of the 1990s, the nations of the world agreed to cut world hunger in half by 2015.

This kind of aid—aid that supports communities and responsible governments—could dramatically reduce world hunger over the next decades. At the UN conferences of the 1990s, the nations of the world agreed to cut world hunger in half by 2015. . . .

Over most of the past 50 years, the U.S. took the lead in advancing foreign aid for developing countries. Foreign-aid priorities were driven by the cold war, and the U.S. saw fighting hunger and poverty as a way to slow communism and woo Third World governments. For example, the biggest recipients of U.S. aid in Africa in the 1980s were dictatorships in Somalia, Sudan and Liberia that contributed to the violence still afflicting these countries today.

Since the end of the cold war, however, funding for aid has dropped. Without a clear statement of purpose for its post-cold-war aid program, Congress has bogged down the work of USAID, the main aid agency within the U.S. government. In the absence of a strong commitment to foreign aid, debilitating myths about such aid have become widespread. Before we sustain a commitment to reducing hunger and poverty around the world, we must debunk these myths.

Myth 1: Foreign Aid Does Not Work

Most foreign aid hasn't helped poor people because it was never intended to help poor people. Over 20 percent of U.S. foreign assistance goes to Israel and Egypt, although neither country is a low-income nation. Other programs in the "aid" budget help U.S. businesses, or underwrite some senator's pet organization back home.

But when aid is focused on reducing poverty, it produces results. In the 1980s, a UNICEF-led "child survival revolution" taught low-income parents worldwide how to do simple things to reduce health risks for their children. A sugar and salt solution, for example, can keep diarrhea from dehydrating a child. Now, in 2001, thousands more children live rather than die each day because of this program.

There are fewer hungry people in the world today than 25 years ago. The proportion of undernourished people in developing countries has dropped from one-third to one-fourth. Since 1960, adult literacy in sub-Saharan Africa has increased by over 280 percent; infant mortality has declined in East Asia by more than 70 percent; the under-five mortality rate has declined by over 75 percent in Latin America and the Caribbean; and life expectancy has risen by 46 percent in South Asia. Development assistance has contributed to these advances.

Myth 2: Aid Gets Lost to Corrupt Bureaucracies

Yes, corruption is a problem. But since the end of the cold war, USAID and other aid agencies have become tougher on corruption. They are selective about which countries receive aid and what local agencies they fund, and they work with governments and nongovernmental organizations (NGOs) to monitor how money is spent. Where corruption is rife, USAID can fund projects through NGOs rather than government agencies.

> *When aid is focused on reducing poverty, it produces results.*

Even more important, people in many developing countries have fought successfully for democracy, so local citizens are better able to hold governments accountable. People can criticize government officials, and the local press discusses mistakes and abuses.

Myth 3: Aid Is a Big Slice of the U.S. Budget

A recent poll by the Program for International Policy Attitudes at the University of Maryland showed that most Americans still imagine that 20 percent of the federal budget goes to foreign aid. In reality, less than 1 percent of the budget is for foreign aid, and only about one-third of that is development assistance.

U.S. development aid has reclined steadily over the past 15 years. The U.S. now ranks last among the 22 industrialized countries in percentage of national income given away in development aid: less than 0.1 percent. Tiny Denmark contributes ten times as much of its national income as American taxpayers do. Japan has been the largest provider of official development assistance for ten consecutive years.

Myth 4: Americans Want to Cut Foreign Aid

This is what members of Congress and their staffers like to tell us. But a University of Maryland study reveals that a vast majority of Americans would support an increase in aid focused on reducing poverty. Eighty-three percent of Americans favor U.S. participation in a plan to reduce world hunger by half by 2015, and nearly all these people would be willing to pay more in taxes to make it happen.

Even more intriguing, U.S. strategic and economic interests, long the prime rationales for U.S. foreign aid, rank last in the minds of Americans as reasons to grant aid. Most believe that alleviating hunger and poverty and encouraging economic development in poor countries are the most compelling reasons for aid.

Myth 5: We Should Take Care of Poverty at Home

Yes, we should tackle hunger and poverty within our own borders. In the U.S., 31 million people—including 12 million children—live in households that don't always have enough food to eat. The U.S. is the only industrialized country that still puts up with widespread hunger within its borders. But as the richest and most prosperous country in the world, we can afford to—and should—both help people here and respond to the needs of people around the world.

In addition, helping people in other countries helps Americans. Rising incomes among people around the world means a more dynamic market for U.S. exports, especially agriculture. U.S. trade with sub-Saharan Africa already exceeds trade with all of the independent states of the former Soviet Union. Development reduces conflict and the costs incurred when the U.S. government responds to crises overseas. Americans also have a self-interest in curtailing communicable diseases such as HIV/AIDS and in preserving rain forests and other environmental resources in poor countries.

Myth 6: Charities Can Take Care of the Poor

Americans give generously to charities such as Catholic Relief Services, Lutheran World Relief, Oxfam and World Vision, and these agencies do excellent, much-needed work. USAID already directs 38 percent of bilateral foreign aid through these and other agencies. Some in Congress would take that a step further: Senator Jesse Helms (R., N.C.) has proposed replacing USAID with a foundation that would channel money to U.S. charities.

> *Helping people in other countries helps Americans.*

But private charities can't do the job alone. The U.S government can mobilize resources on a larger scale, and government-to-government aid can improve public-sector functions that are crucial to making progress against poverty. These include economic policymaking, protection of human rights, and providing public services such as schools and clean water.

Myth 7: Foreign Aid Is Not Important

How countries manage their own resources is much more important than foreign aid. But foreign-aid programs influence how local resources are invested and give a boost to countries that are using their resources well. Some critics claim that the only way to reduce poverty is to restrain capitalism. They see aid programs as a Trojan horse for multinational corporations.

But many developing countries have found that some reliance on free markets stimulates economic growth.

> // We need to expand programs that focus on reducing poverty and that involve poor people as active partners. //

Critics at the other extreme argue, "If these countries would just open their markets, they wouldn't need aid." They point out that international trade and investment are much larger financial flows than aid. But trade and investment tend to bypass poor people. They are no substitute for aid.

A Partnership

We need to expand programs that focus on reducing poverty and that involve poor people as active partners. At the top of the list should be aid to agriculture, because 70 percent of the world's undernourished people live in rural areas. The best agriculture programs listen to local farmers, including women, and involve them directly in agricultural research and extension. We also need to expand programs that fight AIDS. The rapid spread of this disease in Africa is due largely to pervasive poverty, so we must combine the attack on AIDS with a broader attack on poverty.

Programs providing credit to tiny businesses, or microenterprises, are another opportunity. Over the last 20 years, pioneering institutions such as the Grameen Bank have been channeling small loans to very poor people. One key has been the focus on reaching the poor. The other has been the involvement of groups of poor people in order to reduce administrative costs and improve repayment rates.

The international debt relief initiative is an example of effective aid. Protestants, Catholics and others in the Jubilee 2000 campaign have pressed the industrialized-country governments to write off some of the unpayable debt of the world's poorest countries. Churches and Bread for the World's members mobilized an estimated 250,000 letters to Congress in 1999 and 2000. Thanks to this successful advocacy movement, 22 of the world's poorest countries have received $34 billion in debt cancellation. Their debt payments for [2001] have year been reduced $1.1. billion.

In addition, the World Bank and the International Monetary Fund have been instructed to focus on reducing poverty in low-income countries by asking those countries to develop poverty-reduction strategies through processes of public consultation.

Debt relief is working better in some countries than others, but reports are generally encouraging. In Uganda, debt relief has more than doubled primary school enrollment. The public consultation process has also led to innovations that reduce corruption in the education sector. Now, when the Ugandan government disburses money for schools, there are announcements on radio and in newspapers. As a result, corruption in the education sector has dropped from more than 50 percent to less than 10 percent.

Sustained progress against hunger and poverty will require a sustained increase in development assistance. We could cut global hunger in half by 2015 for a U.S. contribution of $1 billion more a year in poverty-focused aid. (One billion dollars is less than one penny per day per American.)

12

Spreading Democracy Will Help Reduce World Poverty

Joseph T. Siegle, Michael M. Weinstein, and Morton H. Halperin

Joseph T. Siegle is an associate director at the Center for Institutional Reform and the Informal Sector at the University of Maryland in College Park. Michael M. Weinstein is director of policy planning and research at the Robin Hood Foundation and an adjunct senior fellow at the Council on Foreign Relations. Morton H. Halperin is director of the Open Society Policy Center and senior vice president at the Center for American Progress. They are the authors of The Democracy Advantage: How Democracies Promote Prosperity and Peace.

Poor democracies generally outperform poor autocracies economically. Democracies also produce better results in terms of quality of life issues such as life expectancy, literacy rates, and access to health services. Low-income democracies are also much better than their autocratic counterparts at avoiding calamities and humanitarian emergencies. Democracies perform better because leaders must respond to the needs of the people, there are checks and balances to avoid governmental malfeasance, and the free flow of information helps nations adapt to changing circumstances. The United States should promote democracy throughout the world.

Joseph T. Siegle, Michael M. Weinstein, and Morton H. Halperin, "Why Democracies Excel," *Foreign Affairs*, vol. 83, September/October 2004, pp. 57–71. Copyright © 2004 by the Council on Foreign Relations. Reproduced by permission.

The empirical evidence is clear: democracies consistently outperform autocracies in the developing world. But before proceeding, it is important to establish what we mean by democracy. Democracies are political systems characterized by popular participation, genuine competition for executive office, and institutional checks on power. . . .

> *On nearly all . . . quality-of-life measures, low-income democracies dramatically outdo their autocratic counterparts.*

Because everyone agrees that the most prosperous states in the world are well-established democracies, and because the real debate is over whether low-income democracies are capable of growing at a rate comparable to that of low-income authoritarian governments, this discussion is limited to countries with GDP [gross domestic product] per capita of under $2,000 (in constant 1995 dollar terms). We thus compare two groups of countries: low-income democracies and low-income autocracies.

The data, compiled from the World Bank's World Development Indicators from 1960 to the present, reveal a simple truth: low-income democracies have, on average, grown just as rapidly as low-income autocracies over the past 40 years. Outside of eastern Asia (about which more will be said later), the median per capita growth rates of poor democracies have been 50 percent higher than those of autocracies. Countries that have chosen the democratic path—such as the Dominican Republic, India, Latvia, Mozambique, Nicaragua, and Senegal—have typically outpaced their autocratic counterparts, such as Angola, the Republic of Congo, Syria, Uzbekistan, and Zimbabwe. Moreover, because 25 percent of the worst-performing authoritarian regimes, including Cuba, North Korea, and Somalia, have failed to document their performance, the growth shortfall for autocracies is even larger than the available data indicate.

Measuring Quality of Life

The advantage poor democracies have over poor autocracies becomes even more apparent when the debate moves from growth rates to broader measures of well-being. Development can also be measured by social indicators such as life expectancy, access to clean drinking water, literacy rates, agricultural yields, and the quality of public-health services. On nearly all of these quality-of-life measures, low-income democracies dramatically outdo their autocratic counterparts.

People in low-income democracies live, on average, nine years longer than their counterparts in low-income autocracies, have a 40 percent greater chance of attending secondary school, and benefit from agricultural yields that are 25 percent higher. The latter figure is particularly relevant because some 70 percent of the people in poor countries live in the countryside. Higher levels of agricultural productivity mean more employment, capital, and food. Poor democracies also suffer 20 percent fewer infant deaths than poor autocracies. Development practitioners should pay particularly close attention to these figures because infant-mortality rates capture many features of social well-being, such as prenatal health care for women, nutrition, quality of drinking water, and girls' education.

> *Careful review of the data suggests that low-income democracies have [a] powerful advantage: they are better at avoiding calamities.*

Careful review of the data suggests that low-income democracies have another powerful advantage: they are better at avoiding calamities. Since 1960, poor autocracies have experienced severe economic contractions (falls of 10 percent or more in annual GDP) twice as often as poor democracies. Seventy percent of autocracies have experienced at least one such episode since 1980, whereas only 5 of the 80 worst examples of economic contraction over the last 40 years have occurred in democracies. . . .

The frequent criticism that democracies pander to populist-driven interests to the overall detriment of the economy is demonstrably false. Poor democracies have, on average, not run higher deficits over the past 30 years than poor autocracies. Similarly, both poor democracies and poor autocracies spend almost the same on education and health. Democracies have just used their resources more effectively. Not coincidentally, low-income democracies typically score between 15 to 25 percent stronger on indices of corruption and rule of law than do autocracies.

Democracies also do a better job of avoiding humanitarian emergencies the 87 largest refugee crises over the past 20 years originated in autocracies, and 80 percent of all internally displaced persons in 2003 were living under authoritarian regimes, even though such systems represented only a third of all states. The Nobel laureate and political economist Amartya Sen once famously observed that no democracy with a free press has ever experienced a major famine.

Some hold that "premature" democratization in low-income countries is responsible for enabling opportunistic politicians to fan ethnic and regional resentments, even armed conflict. According to this point of view, the iron fist of an autocratic leader can keep a fractious society intact. But this argument, too, fails to withstand empirical scrutiny. Poor countries fall into conflict often—about one year in every five since 1980. But poor democratizers fight less frequently than do poor authoritarian nations. In sub-Saharan Africa, where most civil conflict has occurred recently, countries undergoing democratic reform have experienced armed conflict half as often as the norm in the region. . . .

Democracy Works

Having highlighted the superior performance of poor democracies over poor authoritarian regimes, we turn to the conceptual underpinnings of this pattern. Poor democracies outperform authoritarian countries because their institutions enable power to be shared and because they encourage openness and adaptability.

Democratic leaders have incentives to respond to the needs of common citizens. Otherwise, they find themselves out of office. And because ordinary people care about bread-and-butter issues, these concerns figure prominently in candidates' agendas. By contrast, the narrow clan- and patronage-based support on which autocratic leaders often rely for power gives them little incentive to focus on the general well-being of society.

The developmental advantage of democracies also stems from the checks and balances that characterize self-governing political systems. Power is not monopolized by any one individual or branch of government, even though a national leader may claim a popular mandate. Although democracy is a more cumbersome process, it reduces the scope for rash, narrowly conceived, or radical policies that can have disastrous economic consequences. Federated systems also place checks and balances on the various levels of government, thereby guarding against an overconcentration of power at the national level while allowing for flexibility to address local priorities.

> *Democracies also do a better job of avoiding humanitarian emergencies.*

Authoritarian regimes, by comparison, often turn political monopoly into economic monopoly. Only businesses and individuals closely tied to the ruling party are able to acquire the licenses, permits, credit, and other resources needed to succeed. Such preferential treatment diminishes competition and innovation and therefore reduces economic efficiency. Consumers get fewer choices and higher prices. When political allegiances also dictate access to education, housing, career options, and social status, the spectrum of opportunities available to political outsiders is severely narrowed. An integral virtue of democracies, therefore, is that they provide a sphere of private space, which, protected by law, nurtures inventiveness, independent action, and civic activity.

The Open Society

Democracies are open: they spur the flow of information. Organizations in and out of government regularly report findings, educate the public, and push political leaders to consider a full range of options, spreading good ideas from one sector to another. The free flow of ideas, every bit as much as the flow of goods, fosters efficient, customized, and effective policies. Put this way, development is an exercise in educating a population: to wash hands, improve farming techniques, eat nutritious food, or protect the environment, for example. And societies that promote the free flow of information have a distinct advantage in these efforts.

Information is best communicated through multiple and independent channels. For example, it was the active public-education campaign undertaken by the Ugandan government and nongovernmental organizations in the 1990s that dramatically reduced the transmission of HIV/AIDS in that country.

96

Uganda was once the world leader in percentage of adult population infected, at roughly 30 percent, but by 2003, that rate
had declined to 7 percent. By contrast, attempts to suppress information during the SARS epidemic in China allowed the disease to spread before the public became aware and concerted
action could be taken. Once the epidemic was acknowledged,
distrust of the government led many Chinese in infected areas
to violate the government's quarantine. This example also con-
firms a larger proposition: democracies do a better job of cor-
recting errors. Once private or public authorities make decisions in open societies, the results become known and
corrective action, if needed, can be taken.

> *Democracies are open: they spur the flow of information.*

Openness also reduces the scope for corruption. An independent, investigative media creates higher expectations re-
garding transparency and disclosure of potential conflicts of interest. Paradoxically, greater openness in newly democratizing
societies may at first lead to the perception that corruption is
worsening. In Kenya, for example, a survey by Transparency International found that the perception of corruption was worse
in 2003—the first year of the democratically elected government—than in the late 1990s, under the authoritarian rule of
Daniel arap Moi. Yet the same organization found that Kenyans
paid an average of nine bribes in 2003, down from 29 in 2002,
saving roughly 10 percent of their annual income.

Transparency does more than cut the cost of bribes, which,
technically, merely transfer money from one citizen to another
and do not thereby reduce average incomes. The World Bank
estimates that corruption, which acts as a tax on legal commerce and makes returns less certain, costs the global economy
five percent of its total value, or $1.5 trillion a year.

Adapting to Change

Adaptability is another beneficial feature of democracies.
Democracies enhance political stability by establishing clear
mechanisms for succession. This allows them to adapt smoothly

to the death or electoral defeat of a leader, minimizing the scope for extralegal or coercive tactics to attain power. Development momentum is thus sustained even though specific policies change from one administration to the next.

> *// The simple fact is that the West does not tilt its development assistance to democracies. This can and should change. //*

Adherence to established means for transferring power reflects a commitment to the rule of law under a democracy: leaders can gain legitimacy in the eyes of the people only if they ascend to power through democratic processes. Political legitimacy grounded in the rule of law, in turn, provides the foundation for the application of legal norms in the conduct of government and business, and a rules-based regulation of the economy.

Finally, democratic structures adjust well to changing circumstances. Because policies in democracies flow from an elaborate process of trial and error, they can adapt to realities on the ground. When there is a constant flow of policies and ideas, there is pressure to amend, drop, or replace initiatives that do not work. Elections are the most distinctive junctures around which these adjustments occur. But even during a given leader's tenure, constant fine-tuning takes place. Democracies are distinctive, therefore, not because they always identify the best policy but because they institutionalize the right to change leaders or policies when things go poorly. This capacity for revitalization explains why citizens of established nations such as Argentina, Guatemala, Kenya, and South Africa spoke of living in a "new" country after recent democratic changes in leadership.

All in all, then, democracies present an enormously powerful set of institutions that propel development. The more representative, transparent, and accountable those governmental processes, the more likely policies and practices will respond to the basic priorities of the general population.

Promoting Democracy

With the case for supporting democracies so compelling, it may come as a surprise that the United States, other industrialized democracies, and international financial institutions have not shown greater preference to countries on the path to democracy when providing economic assistance. Instead, existing rules have typically prevented democratic criteria from guiding funding decisions. As a result, as much official development assistance (as a percentage of GDP) has been provided to autocracies as to democracies. This is not just a Cold War phenomenon; the same patterns have applied since 1990. Nor does it reflect disproportionate levels of humanitarian assistance to crisis-riven autocracies; the lack of distinction survives even if only non-emergency assistance is considered or the poorest countries are removed from the sample. Despite increased rhetoric and funding for democracy-promotion projects, the simple fact is that the West does not tilt its development assistance to democracies. This can and should change. . . .

Democracy First

We reject a "development first, democracy later" approach because experience shows that democracy often flourishes in poor countries. Moreover, evidence reveals that countries frequently remain poor precisely because they retain autocratic political structures. A development-first strategy thus risks perpetuating the deadly cycle of poverty, conflict, and oppression.

> *We reject a 'development first, democracy later' approach because experience shows that democracy often flourishes in poor countries.*

By contrast, a democracy-centered development strategy presupposes not only that poor countries can successfully democratize but also that democracy brings political checks and balances, responsiveness to citizen priorities, openness, and self-correcting mechanisms—all of which contribute to steady growth and superior living conditions. Establishing domestic institutions that hold leaders accountable to their citizenry; moreover, has the potential to shift the burdens of oversight for development initiatives from international institutions to national political structures. Such a transfer of responsibility would alleviate the administrative burden faced by international agencies and foster development strategies better adapted to local needs.

Alleviating poverty and advancing democracy are long, difficult processes susceptible to periodic setbacks. But these struggles should be contrasted with the incomparably worse hardships frequently suffered under autocracies: economic stagnation, humanitarian crises, and conflict. In helping the developing world rid itself of these scourges, the United States and other industrialized countries must make democracy central to their development agendas.

Organizations to Contact

American Enterprise Institute (AEI)
1150 Seventeenth St. NW, Washington, DC 20036
(202) 862-5800 • fax: (202) 862-7177
e-mail: kstaulcup@aei.org • Web site: www.aei.org

The American Enterprise Institute for Public Policy Research works to pre-serve limited government, private enterprise, and a strong foreign policy through scholarly research, open debate, and publications. Poverty is one of the topics the institute studies. Publications available from AEI's Web site include *Growth and Interaction in the World Economy* and *Poor People's Knowledge: Promoting Intellectual Properly in Developing Countries.*

CARE
151 Ellis St. NE, Atlanta, GA 30303
(404) 681-2552 • fax: (404) 589-2651
e-mail: info@care.org • Web site: www.care.org

CARE is an organization that fights global poverty. The organization conducts fund-raising campaigns to help provide meals for hungry chil-dren. Published articles available from its Web site include "Getting Girls Back to School in Afghanistan" and "South Asia Tsunami Disaster: 100 Days Later."

Cato Institute
1000 Massachusetts Ave. NW, Washington, DC 20001-5403
(202) 842-0200 • fax: (202) 842-3490
e-mail: cato@cato.org • Web site: www.cato.org

The Cato Institute is a libertarian think tank that researches and pro-motes public policies that reduce the role of government. Poverty is one of the issues the institute studies. Publications available from its Web site include *Educational Freedom in Urban America* and *In Defense of Global Capitalism.*

Foundation for Economic Education (FEE)
30 S. Broadway, Irvington-on-Hudson, NY 10533
(800) 960-4FEE • fax: (914) 591-8910
e-mail: fee@fee.org • Web site: www.fee.org

FEE studies the moral and intellectual foundation of a free society and shares its knowledge, including information on poverty, with individu-als everywhere. Publications available from its Web site include *The Mainspring of Human Progress* and *The Freedom Philosophy.*

Heritage Foundation
214 Massachusetts Ave. NE, Washington, DC 20002-4999
(202) 546-4400 • fax: (202) 546-8328
e-mail: info@heritage.org • Web site: www.heritage.org

The Heritage Foundation is a research and educational institute whose mission is to formulate and promote conservative public policies based on the principles of free enterprise, limited government, individual freedom, traditional American values and a strong national defense. Poverty is one of the issues the foundation studies. Its publications include the *2005 Index of Economic Freedom* and *The Road to Prosperity*.

Institute for Research on Poverty
University of Wisconsin–Madison, 1180 Observatory Dr.
3412 Social Science Bldg., Madison WI 53706-1393
(608) 262-6358 • fax: (608) 265-3119
e-mail: evanson@ssc.wisc.edu • Web site: www.irp.wisc.edu

The Institute for Research on Poverty is a center for interdisciplinary research into the causes and consequences of poverty and social inequality in the United States. It is one of three Area Poverty Research Centers sponsored by the U.S. Department of Health and Human Services. Publications available from its Web site include *Poor Kids in a Rich Country: America's Children in Comparative Perspective* and *Race and the Politics of Welfare Reform*.

Joint Center for Poverty Research
Northwestern University
Institute for Policy Research, 2040 Sheridan Rd., Evanston, IL 60208
(847) 491-3395 • fax: (847) 491-9916
e-mail: ipr@northwestern.edu
OR:
University of Chicago
Harris Graduate School of Public Policy Issues, 1155 E. Sixtieth St.,
Chicago, IL 60637
(773) 702-2028 • fax: (773) 702-0426
e-mail: jcpr@uchicago.edu • Web site: www.jcpr.org

The Joint Center for Poverty Research concentrates on the causes and consequences of poverty in America and the effectiveness of policies aimed at reducing poverty. The center's goal is to advance what is known about the economic, social, and behavioral factors that cause poverty, and to establish the actual effects of interventions designed to alleviate poverty. Publications prepared by the center include *How Are Children Affected by Employment and Welfare Transitions?* and *Does It Pay to Move from Welfare to Work?*

National Center for Children in Poverty
215 W. 125th St., 3rd Fl., New York, NY 10027
(646) 284-9600 • fax: (646) 284-9623
e-mail: infor@nccp.org • Web site: www.nccp.org

The National Center for Children in Poverty is part of the Mailman School of Public Health at Columbia University. The center conducts research and publishes information on poverty issues and how they affect children. Publications available from its Web site include *Employment Alone Is Not Enough for America's Low-Income Children and Families* and *Whose Security? What Social Security Means to Children and Families.*

National Poverty Center
Gerald R. Ford School of Public Policy
University of Michigan, 1015 E. Huron St., Ann Arbor, MI 48104-1689
(734) 615-5312 • fax: (734) 615-8047
e-mail: npcinfo@umich.edu • Web site: www.npc.umich.edu

The National Poverty Center promotes research on the causes and consequences of poverty, evaluates and analyzes policies to alleviate poverty, and trains poverty researchers. Video publications available from its Web site include *Why Poor Women Put Motherhood Before Marriage* and *American Dream: Three Women, Ten Kids and a Nation's Drive to End Welfare.*

Poverty & Race Research Action Council (PRRAC)
3000 Connecticut Ave. NW, #200, Washington, DC, 20008
(202) 387-9887 • fax: (202) 387-0764
e-mail: info@prrac.org • Web site: www.prrac.org

PRRAC is a nonpartisan, national, not-for-profit organization convened by major civil rights, civil liberties, and antipoverty groups. The council connects social science research to advocacy work in order to address problems at the intersection of race and poverty. Publications available from its Web site include *Evictions: The Hidden Housing Problem* and *Fragmented: Improving Education for Mobile Students.* The council also publishes the bimonthly newsletter *Poverty & Race.*

U.S. Department of Health and Human Services
Administration for Children and Families
There are ten regional offices throughout the United States of America. Contact information for all ten offices can be found at www.acf.hhs.gov.

The Administration for Children and Families, within the Department of Health and Human Services, supervises federal programs that promote the economic and social well-being of families, children, individuals, and communities. Some of these programs are designed to alleviate poverty. Publications available from its Web site include *A Celebration of the Family* and *State Child Welfare Legislation Report.*

Bibliography

Books

Alberto Alesina and Edward L. Glaeser	*Fighting Poverty in the U.S. and Europe: A World of Difference.* Oxford, UK: Oxford University Press, 2004.
Jagdish Bhagwati	*In Defense of Globalization.* Oxford, UK: Oxford University Press, 2005.
James L. Clayton	*The Global Debt Bomb.* Armonk, NY: M.E. Sharpe, 2000.
Sam Daley-Harris, ed.	*Pathways Out of Poverty: Innovations in Microfinance for the Poorest Families.* Bloomfield, CT: Kumarian Press, 2002.
Sheldon H. Danziger and Robert H. Haveman, eds.	*Understanding Poverty.* Cambridge, MA: Harvard University Press, 2002.
Charles Derber	*People Before Profits: The New Globalization in an Age of Terror, Big Money and Economic Crisis.* New York: St Martin's Press, 2002.
Will Hutton	*A Declaration of Interdependence: Why America Should Join the World.* New York: Norton, 2003.
John Iceland	*Poverty in America: A Handbook.* Berkeley and Los Angeles: University of California Press, 2003.
Robert A. Isaak	*The Globalization Gap: How the Rich Get Richer and the Poor Get Left Behind.* Upper Saddle River, NJ: Prentice-Hall Financial Times, 2005.
John Kay	*Culture and Prosperity: The Truth About Markets; Why Some Nations Are Rich but Most Remain Poor.* New York: HarperCollins, 2004.
Ray Marshall, ed.	*Back to Shared Prosperity: The Growing Inequality of Wealth and Income in America.* Armonk, NY: M.E. Sharpe, 2000.
George McGovern	*The Third Freedom: Ending Hunger in Our Time.* New York: Simon & Schuster, 2001.
Katherine S. Newman	*A Different Shade of Gray: Midlife and Beyond in the Inner City.* New York: New Press, 2003.
Ruby K. Payne	*A Framework for Understanding Poverty.* 3rd rev. ed. Highlands, TX: Aha! Process, 2003.

C.K. Prahalad | *The Fortune at the Bottom of the Pyramid: Eradicating Poverty Through Poverty.* Upper Saddle River, NJ: Wharton School, 2005.

Jeffrey Sachs | *The End of Poverty: Economic Possibilities for Our Time.* New York: Penguin, 2005.

Earl Shorris | *Riches for the Poor: The Clemente Course in the Humanities.* New York: Norton, 2000.

United Nations | *Understanding Poverty from a Gender Perspective.* New York: United Nations, 2004.

Martin Wolf | *Why Globalization Works.* New Haven, CT: Yale University Press, 2005.

Periodicals

Robert Asen | "Including the Poor in the Political Community," *Focus*, Summer 2002.

Haroon Ashraf | "UN Says Global Plan to Help World's Poorest Is Failing Some Nations," *Lancet*, July 12, 2003.

Xavier Bosch | "More Aid Is Needed to Halve World Poverty, Says Report," *Lancet*, May 1, 2004.

John Cassidy | "Always with Us? Jeffrey Sach's Plan to Eradicate World Poverty," *New Yorker*, April 11, 2005.

Barbara Crossette | "Fighting Poverty: Count the U.S. Out," *Humanist*, September/October, 2004.

Economist | "Economic Focus—Ends Without Means," September 11, 2004.

Pete Engardio, Declan Walsh, and Manjeet Kripalani | "Global Poverty: Much Remains to Be Done but Some Programs Have Made Remarkable Gains," *Business Week*, October 14, 2002.

Daphne Eviatar | "Spend $150 Billion per Year to Cure World Poverty," *New York Times Magazine*, November 7, 2004.

Tim Ferguson | "Aid That Works," *Forbes Global*, October 13, 2003.

Mark Hemingway | "Real Business, Real Small," *American Enterprise*, September 2004.

Paul S. Kersey | "Can Southfield Afford a 'Feel-Good' Wage Law?" *Oakland (Michigan) Press*, August 11, 2002.

Zosia Kmietowicz | "Smaller Families Aid Economic Growth, Says UN Report," *British Medical Journal*, December 7, 2002.

Molly Marsh | "Keeping Promises: Will the World Do the Right Thing by Africa?" *Sojourners*, November/December 2003.

Daniel R. Meyer | "Income Support for Children in the United States," *Focus*, Spring 2001.

Bobbi Murray	"Minimum Security: Seeing the Limits of Living-Wage Laws, Activists Seek a Raise for All Workers," *Nation*, July 12, 2004.
James L. Payne	"Why the War on Poverty Failed," *Freeman*, January 1999.
Jeffrey Sachs	"Doing the Sums on Africa," *Economist*, May 20, 2004.
Kristin S. Seefeldt	"Marriage on the Public Policy Agenda: What Do Policy Makers Need to Know from Research?" *Poverty Research Insights*, Winter 2004.
Thomas Sowell	"War on Poverty Revisited," *Capitalism Magazine*, August 17, 2004.
James Traub	"Freedom, from Want," *New York Times Magazine*, February 13, 2005.

Index

108